Good-bye, Pink Pig

GOOD-BYE
PINK PIG

❦

C. S. Adler

G. P. PUTNAM'S SONS
New York

*With thanks to Gloria Schreiber, Learning
Consultant, and Abbot Bernstein, Psychologist, for
their help and information on diagnostic testing, and to
Rose Foster for her help.*

Copyright © 1985 by C. S. Adler
All rights reserved. This book, or parts thereof,
may not be reproduced in any form without permission
in writing from the publishers. Published simultaneously
in Canada by General Publishing Co. Limited, Toronto.
First printing
Printed in the United States of America
Designed by Ellen S. Levine

Library of Congress Cataloging in Publication Data
Adler, C. S. (Carole S.)
Good-bye, Pink Pig.
Summary: Amanda would rather live in a fantasy world
of her imagination than go to her new middle school,
where the custodian is the grandmother she has never met.
1. Children's stories, American.   [1. Imagination—Fiction.
2. Grandmothers—Fiction.   3. Family life—Fiction.
4. Schools—Fiction]   I. Title.   II. Title:
Good-bye, Pink Pig.
PZ7.A26145Go   1985   [Fic]   85-6329
ISBN 0-399-21282-5

For Grayson Daniel Adler,
who has brought us joy just by being.

One

The first person Amanda had seen last spring when her class visited the middle school was Pearly. She had made a dark pillar smack in the center of the lobby for the fifth-graders-to-be to flow around. No question it was Pearly. She was wearing the uniform Amanda's brother Dale had described—black dress with a white collar, and the barrette of pearls that had earned her her nickname pinned the coil of her grayish-brown hair in place. "Hello, angels," Pearly had greeted them loudly.

"Hello, Pearly," the knowing ones had called back. Their older brothers and sisters had told them about the middle school's lady janitor who enforced discipline in the halls and bathrooms and anywhere else she considered her domain. Pearly was a character, a school legend to them, but Amanda had been afraid. She had pressed closer to the wall, trying to hide behind her taller classmates. Still, Pearly's eyes had found her out and fixed on her. How could she follow Mother's instructions not to have anything to do with Pearly, unless—unless Amanda managed not to go to middle school at all.

"She won't bother you," Dale had said. "Just be polite and keep your distance." But Dale had already been a junior in high school last spring, and he was strong, like Mother. Only Pink Pig understood how it felt to be small and weak and scared. Pink Pig was a rose quartz miniature the size of a lima bean who came to life when Amanda needed her.

"I won't know what to say to Pearly," Amanda had confided to Pink Pig.

"You could run away if she talks to you," Pink Pig offered. Her tiny black eyes glistened with sympathy.

"No, the best I can do is get sick and stay home. Will you keep me company if I have to stay alone in the house all day?"

"Oh, yes," Pink Pig said. "Stay home and we'll have fun together." Her broad, soft snout wriggled with enthusiasm.

All summer Amanda had put it out of her mind. She went to day camp and made a wallet for her brother Dale in arts and crafts, a black wallet laced together with red. He said it was just what he needed and jammed the money he was earning at the car wash into it. Late afternoons she walked from the park where day camp was held to the bank and marveled that the tall, elegant lady who sat at a carved desk in the carpeted area and gave people advice about their money was her mother.

"Fine," Amanda always said when Mother asked her how her day had gone. Mother liked to hear things were

8

going well. She had so many problems to deal with, like the car's worn brakes, and the aged furnace that wouldn't last another winter, not to mention the dentist bills for capping Dale's teeth, and the ongoing problem of what to do with Amanda while Mother worked.

"Going to camp will be good for you," Mother had promised. "You need to develop your social skills and get outdoors more." Instead day camp turned out dreadful. The counselor didn't know what to do with her charges and let them run wild and fight with each other. Amanda protected herself by staying back, quiet as a mouse, but she never told Mother that. First of all, she knew Mother had no place else to send her, and secondly, Mother disapproved of mouselike behavior.

"Being quiet and shy won't get you anywhere, Amanda. You're so small that people can overlook you too easily. You must stand tall, speak up and make yourself noticed," Mother had often instructed her.

"Little Mouse," Dale used to call her affectionately until Mother caught him at it and told him he was encouraging the wrong behavior in his sister.

Labor Day came and school started. Amanda had been glad not to have to go to day camp anymore. All she had gotten out of it was a bad cold.

"But she can't stay home from school alone," Mother had said to Dale. "And a cold isn't worth my taking personal days for. *Why* couldn't Amanda's baby-sitter have waited a few years before she retired to Florida!"

"Amanda doesn't mind being alone," Dale had said. "She'll entertain herself fine with her books and miniatures. She's not going to get in any trouble."

Mother had called the middle school and promised to

get a note from Amanda's doctor if she was home for more than a few days. Also, Mother and Dale had invented a safety system. Amanda was to answer the phone or the door while she was alone only if the caller rang twice, hung up or paused, then rang again.

The cold lasted a week. "You don't have a fever, but if you're still not feeling well, we'd better take you to the doctor," Mother said. She looked anxious, either because she would have to take time off from work or because of the expense of a doctor's examination, Amanda thought. Mother worried a lot about money. She was always fretting over whether she should put more of it away for Dale's college costs or whether she could spend it on tickets for the concert series or her latest antique-shop find. The doctor said Amanda appeared to be healthy, but keeping her home another day or two wouldn't hurt if she still felt weak.

"I'll be well tomorrow," Amanda had said. She had said it twice now and each time Mother's frown had lasted longer.

The maple on the corner next to the big stone church showed a flash of scarlet leaves. It always led the way for the trees that filled the sky in front of their tiny house. Dale said the house was cramped, but Mother called it a little gem because it was a hundred and seventy years old and had a fanlight over the door and beams in the living room ceiling and a slate roof. She loved it even though it was close to the shabby downtown main street and derelicts wandered through the neighborhood so that it was dangerous for little girls to walk around alone.

"You're faking it, aren't you, Mouse?" Dale asked her

privately one morning before he left for school. He had Mother's curved-in cheeks and black hair and blue eyes, while Amanda had inherited her father's colorlessness. At least that's what Mother said. Amanda had never seen her father because he'd left them after she was born and Mother had torn up all her pictures of him.

"I just don't feel right," Amanda told Dale. She wasn't lying. Every time she thought of facing Pearly, her stomach gave a squeeze of fear which certainly didn't feel right.

"You're not scared of going to a new school?" he asked her.

"Not much," she said. "Libby's there. Libby called me and asked me when I'm coming. She says Mr. Whittier isn't going to let her save me a seat forever."

"Yeah," he said. "I guess you wouldn't leave your friend Libby stranded unless you were really sick."

"I just don't feel right," she repeated, and she would have told him about Pearly if he hadn't shrugged and smiled and said she'd better get well soon.

After Dale left, Amanda retrieved Pink Pig from under her pillow. Pink Pig came alive, but remained tiny enough to fit into Amanda's hand. Staying small kept Pink Pig safe. If anyone came upon them unexpectedly, she could instantly become a rose quartz miniature again instead of the magical talking, thinking creature who was Amanda's dearest friend. "Today," Amanda said, "let's put on Mother's *Swan Lake* tape and dance."

"What a good idea!" Pink Pig agreed. She was always ready for fun. "But will you have room with all the furniture?"

"I'll make room." Amanda pushed the coffee table to

11

one side of the pale blue velvet couch. That left a small square of space on the Chinese rug between the built-in bookcases on the fireplace wall and the two bowlegged armchairs that stood in front of the curtain that screened off Amanda's bedroom area. After she cleared Mother's cloisonné collection from the coffee table so that Pink Pig could dance there, Amanda tried an experimental *grand battement.* Her kick knocked a lampshade crooked.

"We'd have more room to dance in my world," Pink Pig said. "And there we could invite Ballerina to dance with us."

Pink Pig was right. Besides, everything was more fun in the Little World. Holding Pink Pig, Amanda closed her eyes and waited for her friend to transport her. In the Little World, Amanda would become miniature size, bigger than Pink Pig, but still small enough to move easily among the creatures there.

When Amanda opened her eyes, she was standing in the deserted village square below the castle on the hill, where Wizard lived hidden in veils of mist. Ballerina came running out of one of the cottages that surrounded the square wearing her pink tutu and her satin toe shoes. She did a *plié* and posed, waiting for the right note to enter the music. Off they went, all three, with Pink Pig on her hind legs, dipping and twirling as the sound rose and curled and fell and rose again around them. Ballerina was totally absorbed in her dancing, but following her complex movements was easy for Amanda. She felt wonderful as she glided gracefully around the hard-packed dirt of the village square.

Strange that she had been self-conscious and clumsy

12

when Mother had taken her to ballet lessons last year. Perhaps the teacher's instructions had gotten in the way, Amanda reasoned. She remembered Mother saying hopefully, "You're small and thin enough to be a ballet dancer. Maybe *that's* what you have talent for." Mother had been so disappointed when the ballet teacher had assigned Amanda to the back row at the recital, where no one could see her. Unfortunately, Amanda often disappointed Mother. Even Dale did sometimes, as when the highest marks on his report cards were Bs.

"I'm out of breath!" Pink Pig cried. She plunked her forefeet on the ground, breathing hard. "My legs are too short for all that bending and stretching."

"Then we'll stop," Amanda said. She made a reverence to Ballerina, who bowed back and ran off into her house. "What shall we do next?"

"Snooze in the sun?" Pink Pig suggested. It was her favorite activity. She glanced up at the castle. "The mist seems thinner, doesn't it? I hope Wizard isn't getting tired of changing things inside his castle."

"What would happen if he is?"

"I don't know, but Frog says Wizard could cause a lot of trouble if he ever started changing things down here." Pink Pig studied the hilltop where sections of the castle's stone wall showed clearly.

"Why don't you take your snooze, and I'll go back to my own world and read for a while," Amanda said. "We can go to Peasant Man and Peasant Woman's farm together later."

Amanda opened her eyes in her own living room and set off to find her library book. There it was on her dresser, just below the miniature shelf. Near Pink Pig,

13

who was back in her station on the shelf, stood the glazed china figurine of a ballerina balancing gracefully on one slender leg. On the shelf, Wizard was just a tiny pewter man in a pointy gray hat and a flowing beard and cloak. Mother had given him to Amanda, along with the pewter knights and the dragon. Mother liked pewter. Boy with the Guitar was pewter too, but he'd been a gift from Dale. Most of the forty-odd miniatures Amanda owned came from Mother or Dale. The rest had arrived anonymously in the mail on her birthdays. Pink Pig had come first, on Amanda's fifth birthday, but who had sent her was a mystery.

Amanda was still lying on her bed reading when the telephone signal came, two rings, a pause and another ring. Her screened-off bedroom was deep in late afternoon shadows cast by the big trees that lined the street. Dale should have come home by now, and she wasn't surprised that he was the one who was calling.

"Manda, I'm at the pizza parlor with some guys," he said. "Can you cover for me if Mother gets home before I do?"

"What should I say?"

"Say I went out on some business and will be right back. You okay?"

"I'm fine," she said, although it was the time of day when she got what she thought of as the lonelies.

"Thanks, sweetheart," he told her. "You're the best."

To give herself something to do until Mother got home at six, Amanda set the table. Then she switched on the television in the bookshelf in the living room. News—the world was full of accidents and people getting hurt and hurting each other. On the program

14

meant for children, a car was hurtling over a cliff. She flicked off the television and took Pink Pig from the shelf.

In a wink they were in the Little World where it was always pleasant. The sun shone, and a breeze fanned the lacy leaves of trees that edged the open fields along the winding road into the far distance beyond Peasant Man and Peasant Woman's farm. Pink Pig took her into the bare room where Peasant Man and Peasant Woman slept in a high wooden bed and ate at a wooden table and cooked over an open fire.

"Watch out," Pink Pig cried and fell over onto her roly-poly back as Cat scooted past chasing a red yarn ball that unwound in a maze beneath the wooden table between Amanda's feet, across Peasant Woman's empty slippers, under the wooden bed and straight across Pink Pig. Pink Pig squealed and churned the air with all four stubby legs. Cat ran the yarn across Pink Pig's snout. That neatly tied one of Pink Pig's beautiful translucent ears across her eye.

"You look like a pirate pig," Amanda said, giggling as she unwound the yarn from Pink Pig's corkscrew tail. The yarn crisscrossed the dirt floor of the cottage like a red spider web.

By the time Mother's key clicked in the lock, Amanda was back in her own bedroom, and Cat with the Ball of Yarn sat in its station on the miniature shelf, just a gray-and-white painted ceramic miniature with a red ball of yarn forever in its mouth.

"Mother's going to be mad that Dale's not home," Amanda whispered to Pink Pig, who nestled comfortingly warm and rubbery in Amanda's palm.

15

"Amanda, where are you?" Mother called. "Good heavens, what's happened to the living room? Who moved all the furniture around?" She set the lampshade straight and immediately began putting the room in order. Then she looked at Amanda, who was standing in the opening to her room biting her lip anxiously. "Why are you there in the dark?"

"I like the dark," Amanda said.

"Amanda, don't be silly. Nobody likes the dark." As she talked, Mother continued moving around snapping on lights. Her collection of old locks sprang into view on the wall above the couch, complete with the misshapen shadows that Amanda used to imagine were gnomes watching her. Soon the room was brighter than it ever got during the day. "Where's Dale? Did he leave you alone here all afternoon again?"

The clock from Lucerne chimed on the mantel. "He'll be back in a minute. He just went out for something," Amanda said.

"Did *he* mess up the living room?"

"No, I did," Amanda said. "I'm sorry."

"What on earth were you doing?"

"Just playing."

Mother pressed her fingers against her temples. She looked so tired. The frown lines were double dents between her eyes, and though her eyes were still vivid blue moons, half-moon shadows underlined them.

"Shall I bring you some aspirin?" Amanda asked.

"No, thank you. I'm not sick. And you must be feeling well too, or you wouldn't have had the energy to rearrange all the furniture for whatever you were playing. School tomorrow?"

16

"I don't know," Amanda said doubtfully.

"Come here and let me feel your head."

Amanda submitted her high narrow forehead to Mother's cool fingers. She closed her eyes and leaned slightly against Mother's hand. The last time she'd been sick enough to stay home from school, really sick with a high fever, Mother had put cool wet washcloths on her head and brought her drinks with ice in them. She had read Amanda a story too, *Winnie the Pooh*. Amanda had been in kindergarten then. She'd still been sick in bed on her birthday. That was when Pink Pig arrived in the mail, and Dale had said the miniature came from Amanda's fairy godmother. Being sick was nice, Amanda thought. Too bad she would have to give it up now.

"Dale shouldn't have gone out and left you here alone," Mother fretted.

"He knew I'd be all right," Amanda said.

"You shouldn't make excuses for him," Mother said. "We spoil him, you and I. Well, he is a charmer, isn't he?" She touched Amanda's wispy hair. "You never brush it. Don't you want to make it grow thick and silky like Mother's? Bring me your hairbrush, darling."

Obediently Amanda got the brush with the pink rosebuds painted on it, and Mother began a rhythmic stroking. Amanda stood enjoying the fuss Mother was making over her even though she knew it wouldn't transform her into the beautiful little girl Mother wanted.

"Where *is* that boy?" Mother said after a few minutes. "I was going to make a soufflé for his dinner, but it'll be too late to start soon. This whole day has been nothing but one frustration after another." She put the brush down. "Be a dear and bring me a glass of mineral water with a slice of lime in it. I'll just lie down and relax with some chamber music till he comes."

Amanda hastened to oblige. Six-twenty according to the clock in the kitchen. Dale was really late. Amanda had to stand on a chair to get the ice cubes from the freezer. From there she could see over the top of the kitchen curtain. Dale was running down the alley lined with garages that was behind their house. He vaulted their back fence. He'd come in happy. Spending time with his friends made him happy. He didn't get to socialize because he had studying to do and sports practice to attend so that he'd be a star and get a scholarship to a fine college. That was what Mother wanted, and Dale wanted it too—to please Mother.

The hollow, stringy sound of the chamber music covered the squeak of the back door. "What'd you tell her, Mouse?" Dale whispered.

"What you said."

"Good girl. I knew I could count on you." He kissed the top of her head and took the glass from her hand. Then he sauntered into the living room.

"There you are, Mrs. Bickett," he said presenting the glass to Mother with a flourish. "And how's the beautiful executive lady banker feeling this evening?"

"Frazzled," she said. "Giving financial advice to people who don't understand what I'm talking about is tedious. My smile begins to crack around the edges by mid-afternoon. Where were you, Dale?"

"Taking care of business." He bent and kissed her cheek. "Want me to massage your neck?"

"Oh, would you, darling?" She sounded grateful, but

she added faintly, "You shouldn't leave Amanda alone so long."

"What's another couple of hours? She doesn't mind, Mother."

Mother sighed and didn't argue. Amanda was glad. She liked it when they were peaceful together. Besides, Dale was right. She was ten years old and could watch after herself perfectly well.

Libby called that evening and demanded, "When're you coming to school?"

"Tomorrow," Amanda said.

"You better," Libby said. "There's a new girl in our class who wants to be friends with us. And we finished reviewing and we start the new stuff in math next. Besides, I miss you, Amanda."

Amanda was touched. From Libby, "I miss you" meant a lot.

Amanda was lying in bed looking out at the streetlamp moon that shone through the leaves of the tree at the curb in front of the house. To see the real moon, she would have to wait until the leaves fell.

"Manda," Dale whispered through her curtain. "You awake?"

"Yes," she said.

He came in and sat at the end of her bed. "Well, I figured it out," he said. "It's Pearly, isn't it? She's why you don't want to go to middle school."

"I'm going."

"That's what you've been saying for the past week and a half."

"She looked at me," Amanda confided. "She looked right at me as if she knew who I was."

"Sure she knows who you are," Dale said. "She's your grandmother, silly."

"But I won't know what to say to her."

"She won't bother you. Mother can't stand her, but Pearly's not such a bad character. The main thing is to ignore it if kids tease you about her."

"I don't care about teasing," Manda said truthfully.

"Then what are you scared of?"

Amanda was silent. She couldn't explain it to him better than she already had. She remembered that once Dale had pointed Pearly out to her in the supermarket. Pearly had been pushing a shopping cart like anybody else, a spry-looking lady with a sturdy body and plump cheeks and a sausage nose. "She doesn't look mean," Amanda had said doubtfully to Dale.

"She's not mean. After Dad walked out on us, Pearly even came to ask if we needed help. But she and Mother had a big fight and she told Mother off, and Mother's never forgiven her, that's all. Besides, Mother says Pearly's common."

"Common?"

"That means Mother thinks she's loud and not ladylike. But you don't have to be afraid of her, Manda."

The next morning when Amanda walked into the kitchen for breakfast, Mother and Dale were discussing Pearly. Mother and brother sat tall and slim in their chairs at opposite sides of the table, arched eyebrows over startling blue eyes and the same dark hair and curved-in cheeks mirroring each other. "You never told me they teased you about Pearly," Mother said to Dale.

20

"It was no big deal," Dale said. "Anyway, it wasn't her fault kids found out. Bickett's not that common a name, and when they asked me if she was a relative, I admitted she was my grandmother. So what?"

"I should have changed the name legally," Mother said. "I could have used my maiden name, but I never thought we'd stay here. If the bank hadn't promoted me, we'd have moved long ago to a city with more culture than this backwater offers. Bickett. Even the sound is ugly."

"Well, you're not going to change anything this morning," Dale said. He grinned at Amanda. "Feeling okay now?"

"Yes," Amanda said. She couldn't stay home forever, after all.

"Thatta girl." He gave her a hug and a quick kiss before he raced off, late as always for his early morning class.

"Would you like me to drive you to school, Amanda?" Mother asked. She was wearing her gray suit with the diamond stickpin in her ascot tie. Amanda wanted to compliment her the way Dale did, but the words trickled back down her throat. She had never been able to talk to Mother. It was hard to find the right words, and Mother was too impatient to listen very long, or if she seemed to be listening, she didn't understand, and if she understood, she didn't like what she heard.

"I can wait at the bus stop," Amanda offered so that Mother wouldn't risk being late for work.

"Hurry," Mother told her. Amanda put her lunch money in the zippered pocket of her new notebook. She slipped Pink Pig into her jacket pocket.

21

"Try to smile, Amanda," Mother said. "People like you better if you smile at them." She gave a brilliant sample of a people-winning smile.

Amanda tried to imitate it, but Mother sighed and shook her head. "Never mind," she said. "Just remember. If that woman says anything to you, be polite, but keep your distance."

Amanda nodded. Her heart was pumping madly. On the bus she cupped Pink Pig in her hand so that none of the children on the seats around her could see. Pink Pig snuggled cozily in Amanda's palm. Her black-speck eyes were shiny with sympathy, and the translucent pink ears curved forward attentively. "I'm scared," Amanda admitted.

"I'll stick by you," Pink Pig said, and Amanda felt comforted.

Two

Amanda's bus was the last to pull up to the curb. She followed the stream of children who dashed or strolled or trudged into the two-story-high tan brick building, but scary thoughts skittered through her mind. Suppose Mr. Whittier was angry at her for missing the first two weeks of the term. Suppose she was too far behind to catch up and got sent back to fourth grade. Or suppose Libby had had to give her seat away and they couldn't sit together. Inside the open glass doors, Amanda faced a long, unfamiliar hallway and a stairway to her left.

"How am I going to find my homeroom?" Amanda whispered to Pink Pig, who was hidden in Amanda's shirt pocket so they could speak without being noticed.

"Ask someone," Pink Pig said.

"Please!" Amanda stopped a tall, thin girl carrying a potted plant. "Where's Mr. Whittier's room?"

"Upstairs and to your left," the girl said impatiently, and hurried on with her errand.

Amanda didn't remember climbing the stairs on her class visit. She hoped she had the right school. Nothing was looking at all familiar. Except the library. At the top of the stairs she saw the library flanked by bulletin boards across the hall to her right. The library with its display of new books and its inviting round white table and cushioned chairs reassured her, even though everyone passing her looked very large. She knew that middle school went from fifth to eighth grade, but she hadn't expected to be the smallest person in the whole building except for Libby. Getting sent back to elementary school seemed more likely all the time.

"Just take a deep breath and keep going," Pink Pig said.

A lean gray-haired man was standing at a desk piled high with papers, reading something. He looked up at Amanda when she stepped into his room. Dale said Mr. Whittier was nice, but he didn't look very welcoming. From the corner of her eye, Amanda saw a room packed with desks. Each desk had a body, but no body looked like Libby's. "If you're from the office," Mr. Whittier growled, "you can tell them they'll get their forms when they allow me time to fill them out."

"I'm Amanda Bickett," Amanda said.

"Amanda!" Libby squealed. "Over here by the closet."

"Aha!" Mr. Whittier said. "Our long-lost class member appears. Fortunate that you're small since we're already short of space. Well, welcome to fifth grade. No doubt Libby will see you get what you need." He returned to his reading.

24

Dismissed, Amanda looked around. His homeroom certainly looked relaxed. Kids were sitting on desks. Kids were eating their lunch, although it was barely past breakfast time. Kids were writing insults and playing games on the chalkboard and talking to each other and laughing.

"Chin up," Mr. Whittier said, misinterpreting her slowness to move. "They may look ferocious, but none of them bites—so far as I know."

Libby came to claim her, linking arms with Amanda to lead her to a desk with a permanently attached chair in a nook toward the back of the room. "Vera wanted to sit here, but I said we've sat next to each other since third grade. So she made Mr. Whittier move three other people to let her sit behind us. Isn't it nice we don't have to sit in the front, Amanda?"

"Nice," Amanda agreed. They had always been assigned front seats because of their size. Mr. Whittier apparently didn't care if they couldn't see the chalkboard. There didn't seem to be anything on it but jokes and scribbles anyway. "Who's Vera?"

"Didn't I tell you? She's the new principal's daughter. She sat with Pam's group the first week, and then with Karen and Betsy last week, and this week it's you and me."

"Do you like her?"

"Well—not especially. But she's got to have someone to sit with."

Amanda smiled. Libby couldn't imagine anyone content to be alone. Her life was so meshed with the activities of her seven brothers and sisters that school was the closest she came to being free to do what she wanted without considering other people's needs. Libby thought

25

it was because Amanda didn't have time that she and Libby rarely saw each other outside of school. She didn't suspect that Amanda's mother didn't like her because the one time she had come to Amanda's house, Libby had eaten with her mouth open, talked too much and used the wrong word about going to the bathroom.

"People judge you by your friends, Amanda," Mother had said afterward. "You don't want to associate with a girl who has no manners."

"Libby's kind and she likes me," Amanda had said.

As usual Mother didn't listen. "Think about it," she said. "You'll see I'm right."

What Amanda thought was that she'd better not invite Libby for another visit. Then, after the one time Mother allowed Amanda to spend an afternoon at Libby's house, Mother had asked questions. "Libby's mother is a *potter* and her father's looking for a job? With eight children, they must be in terrible straits. Is their house clean, at least?"

"I think so," Amanda said. "I didn't notice."

"Well, what did you have for lunch?"

"Tomato soup and peanut-butter sandwiches."

"And what did you play?"

"We played with the babies. Libby showed me how to put a diaper on, and I held a bottle for the littlest one. Oh, and we gave them a bath."

Mother raised an eyebrow. "In other words Libby's mother used you as a free baby-sitter." She shook her head.

"I like Libby," Amanda had protested.

"That's not the point," Mother had said. "Forming the right associations makes all the difference in life.

Look at Dale. Everyone he brings home comes from a good family. Amanda, if I had known how important background is, I'd never have married your father and had to struggle so hard to give you and Dale the advantages you have. Believe me, I'm not being mean, darling. I'm telling you this for your own good."

Mother meant what she said, but Amanda wasn't convinced. She couldn't help thinking that she wouldn't have been born if Mother had not married Roland Bickett. As for Dale, he only brought home those friends he knew would measure up to Mother's standards. Lately, in fact, he hadn't brought anybody home. No, even though she wanted very much to please Mother, Amanda wouldn't give up Libby.

The review test on last year's math work seemed easy, and Ms. Hart, the gentle young English teacher with very long hair, said, "Libby tells me you're quite the writer, Amanda. Today's free writing period. I'm looking forward to seeing your work."

Amanda was deciding what to write about for Ms. Hart when a bulky girl with glasses and a square face came in and sat down behind Libby. "How was it?" Libby asked her.

"Not so bad," the girl said. "He only filled one."

"Vera had to go to the dentist today," Libby said to Amanda about the large girl. Then remembering they didn't know each other, Libby turned around to tell Vera, "This is Amanda. She finally came."

"Hi," Vera said without smiling. She looked at Amanda critically. "Another shrimp," she said. "You're even shorter than Libby."

"She's not shorter than me, just thinner," Libby said

27

loyally. "Vera is good at math, Manda. Between the three of us we'll be good at everything." Libby smiled happily at the thought and added, "Vera wants to be an actress. Maybe you could write a play for her."

"I want to be a director or a producer, not an actress," Vera corrected.

They had to be quiet then because Ms. Hart sat down on her desk and began to explain that free writing was a wonderful chance to express the things that mattered most to you, and that this week she hoped they wouldn't write rehashes of television programs they'd seen or blow-by-blow accounts of their summer vacation trips. "Let your imaginations go," she said. "Just write whatever comes into your head and don't worry about it. If it doesn't sound good, you don't have to show it to anybody, not even to me."

Amanda fingered Pink Pig who was in her pocket and began her story:

One day Pink Pig went for a walk through the green and gold forest. Leaves were falling from the trees like a golden rain. Pink Pig rolled on her back in the leaves and one landed on her nose. "Are you my friend?" Pink Pig asked the leaf. The leaf didn't answer. "I wish I had a friend," Pink Pig said. "If I had a friend, I wouldn't be lonely, and I'd never be bored because I'd have somebody to do things with."

"I'll be your friend," a voice said.

Pink Pig looked around, but all she saw were tree trunks and falling leaves. She listened. Then she said, "Who are you?"

28

"Nobody much," the voice said. "But I could be your true friend if you want me."

Then Pink Pig looked down and there beside her, crawling on a golden leaf, was a caterpillar, the brown and black, furry kind. "You look nice," Pink Pig said.

"Me? I'm just a lowly caterpillar. So do you want me to be your friend?"

"Yes," Pink Pig said. She was happy to go walking through the green and gold forest with the caterpillar riding on her head. Well, spring came and the caterpillar turned into a butterfly. Then everybody said how lucky Pink Pig was to have such a beautiful friend.

Amanda read the story over to herself and worried that it was too simple, that Ms. Hart would think it was silly. She changed some words and crossed out others. She was still dissatisfied, but since she didn't have time left to create another story, she copied that one over onto a clean page.

When she was finished, she looked at Vera, who was still writing, and at Libby, who was folding an origami bird. She'd been making the same bird for years, always glad to give away what anyone wanted. Between the two of them, Libby had the most to offer a friend, Amanda thought. Libby was kind and loving and lively. While Amanda was too nothing—too small, too plain, too quiet. No wonder Mother was dissatisfied with her. Mother liked only old and beautiful things or a special person like Dale.

Even the senior vice-president of her bank who had taken Mother out for dinner a few times, and for whom she'd bought a soft, low-necked dress, didn't please her for long. As for the women in her businesswomen's club, Mother said they were not to be trusted, and she called the people she worked with on boards and committees either dull or snobbish. When she went to a concert or the theater, she took Dale and Amanda as companions. Mother said she was too busy raising her children to have time for personal friends.

Ms. Hart was looking over her shoulder and reading what Amanda had written.

"Libby was right," Ms. Hart said, "you're very imaginative, Amanda. How about reading this to the class?"

"Oh, no!" Amanda said.

Libby promptly offered to read the story for her. She usually did the reading when Amanda was asked to share. From long years of practice, she had no trouble following Amanda's small pointy handwriting. When she finished reading the short piece, Libby looked around the class expectantly, but nobody said anything. "Wasn't it good?" Libby asked Vera.

"Okay if you go for fairy tales," Vera said. She read her own story aloud next. It was about a gory murder in a shack on a riverbank, and it had a lot of blood in it. Amanda was glad it didn't sound believable enough to give her the shivers.

"Next time we have free writing, let's ask Hart if we can write a play together; I bet she'd let us," Vera said as they were walking down the hall to their next class.

"That'd be fun," Libby said. "And we could act it out." She looked at Amanda and added considerately, "If we did it with puppets, you could do it, Manda. Remember the puppet show we did last year?"

"Sure," Amanda said. Hidden behind a curtain, she hadn't been too shy to act a part.

At lunch Vera moved over so Amanda could squeeze onto the bench beside her. Vera might not make such a bad friend, Amanda thought.

She'd completely forgotten Pearly until she walked out of the girls' bathroom after lunch and saw Pearly in the hall. Amanda grabbed for Pink Pig, then froze and watched.

Pearly was blocking the door of the boys' bathroom. She stood with feet apart and hands on hips lecturing two big boys trying to get out, eighth graders surely. One even had a mustache while the other had a silly grin.

"You wanna smoke, find somewheres beside my bathrooms. I got enough trouble keeping them clean without you stinking them up with smoke." Pearly's voice was loud, as if she didn't care who heard her.

"We wasn't smoking," the mustached one said. "Was we, Gary?"

"No way. Pearly just wants to get us in trouble."

"Not as much trouble as you're giving yourselves. You're going to ruin your lungs," Pearly said.

"Come on, Pearly. You're making us late to gym, and *you* can't give us a pass to Mr. K, can you?" Gary asked slyly.

"All you can get from Mr. K is detention," Pearly said. "You get lung cancer from smoking and that's a lot worse."

"Can it," the mustached boy told Pearly. "We don't need to take nothing from *you*."

Instantly Pearly grabbed him by the ear. "March," she said. "I told you next time you mouthed off to me,

31

you'd land in the principal's office. Think I don't mean what I say?"

The trio moved down the hall with Gary hanging over Pearly's shoulder, pleading for his friend who was complaining, "Ow, you're hurting me. Let go. Ow, Pearly. You let go of me." Amanda shuddered, hoping that Pearly had been too busy to notice Amanda watching her.

All in all, it had been a better day than she expected. Amanda felt cheerful until she reached for the house key in the zipper section of her notebook where she also kept pens, her lunch money and change for an emergency phone call. The key wasn't there. Suddenly she remembered Dale had lost his and borrowed hers. While she'd been sick it hadn't mattered, but he'd forgotten to get another one made and here she was locked out. She tried the bell without much hope that he'd be home. Soccer practice was every afternoon after school. "How does she expect me to win a sports scholarship if I don't go to practice?" Dale had grumbled when Mother said he must get home early for Amanda's sake. It was true Mother wasn't always logical. When she wanted two things equally and couldn't have them both, she didn't make a choice; she just kept wanting.

Amanda sat down on the front step and set Pink Pig on her knee to talk over the day with her. Pink Pig agreed that Vera might not be so bad, and that anyway, it was better to have two friends so that one was always available even if the other had a dentist's appointment. Besides, as a loyal friend, Amanda had to try and like whomever Libby liked.

A lady walked by with a small gray poodle and a large

32

black one on leashes. She smiled at Amanda. Amanda smiled back and moved behind the bushy yew beside the steps, where she couldn't be seen from the street.

"Dale should come soon," Amanda said. He didn't though. A car passed by with flowers painted all over its doors and a bumblebee painted on its hood. A lady with skinny legs and socks hanging over men's boots wandered by mumbling to herself. She slapped the air in front of her as if she were hitting someone and slapped it again. Luckily the lady didn't see Amanda behind the bush.

If Vera became a friend, Amanda could bring her home. Mother might like her better than Libby because Vera's father was the principal. Also, Vera kept her mouth closed when she chewed. Amanda had noticed that because at lunch Vera had told Libby, "You're supposed to keep your mouth closed when you eat."

"Ha-ha," Libby said, thinking Vera was joking. "How do you get the food in then?"

"After you get it in, you chew with your mouth closed. Like this," Vera had said and demonstrated. Libby had looked embarrassed then and Amanda had felt bad for her.

Darkness slipped under the trees. A lamp was lit in the curtainless window of the house across the way. Roomers stayed in that house. One of them was crazy. Amanda hoped the crazy one didn't start breaking windows and screaming again. It was scary when he screamed. A black dog sniffed along the curbside. It had a mean, tail-down look, and when it looked toward Amanda, it stopped. Amanda stiffened, but instead of coming toward her, the dog bent its head and continued to the red fire hydrant halfway down the street. The street lamp on the corner turned on. Amanda felt

33

cramped. She thought of all her math homework. Perhaps she should have tried to do it out here. Too late, now that it was dark. "I'm sorry, Pink Pig," she said to her patient friend. "I'm very sorry we can't go inside."

"Dale will come soon," Pink Pig assured her.

The heels plicking down the sidewalk sounded familiar. Mother must have parked her car near the church again. Amanda squat-walked to the other side of the bush so that Mother wouldn't see her from the front step when she unlocked the door. Mother went inside.

Now Dale would have to make up a story about how he'd taken Amanda with him somewhere—the library maybe. He often said he'd taken her to the library. Mother never checked to see if they had new books with them. Amanda considered allowing herself to be seen and letting Dale explain his way out of trouble without her help. But then Mother would be unhappy and the whole evening would be arguments. She sighed and waited.

"Dale!" Amanda hissed when she finally saw him. He didn't hear her. He was coming around the corner with another boy, a hairy-looking boy with big shoulders. Mother didn't like beards or metal-studded bracelets like the one the boy was wearing below his rolled-up sleeves. They were standing on the corner talking. Amanda ran across the street hoping Mother wasn't watching. Once she reached the corner, they'd be out of sight from the house. Dale reached out an arm and pulled her against him.

"My little sister, Manda," he said to the boy, who said "Hi" and went on talking.

"You gotta believe it's a bargain, Dale. Would I lie to you?"

"I'm sure it's a bargain, but where'd I put a motorcycle even if I could afford one?"

"Come on. There's gotta be space you could rent around here. Come to the meet with me Saturday anyways. You gotta see Big Henry. I told you about him. He's outrageous."

"You know, I'd like to, but I've got a game Saturday."

"So what if you miss one. Jeez, you're only young once, you know. Come on, break loose and live a little. My sister's gonna be there."

"Yeah?" Dale got a funny smile on his face. "I just might," he said. "Listen, you go make your delivery, and I'll catch you in school tomorrow. Okay?"

"Gotcha," the boy said. He grinned at Amanda, turned and clomped off in his heavy boots.

"Is he your friend?" Amanda asked Dale.

"Sure. He's a character. You should hear the stories he tells."

"Mother wouldn't like him."

"Mother wouldn't like most of my friends. . . . Did you wait outside for me all this time?"

"Yes. You forgot to give me back my key. What will we tell her?"

"I'm sorry, Manda." He dug out her key and returned it to her with an apologetic hug. "I didn't mean to be so late. The guys wanted me to go for a hamburger, and I can't always say no. Rats!" He shook his head in disgust. "How about that I took you along to visit a sick friend?"

Mother believed him. Mother almost always believed him. "What I can't understand is why you never remember to leave me a note. You know how I worry when you and Amanda aren't home when I arrive."

"I was sure we'd be back in time, Mom," Dale said. "Come on, don't be mad. Give me a smile to brighten my day, please?"

Mother smiled. Dale could always win her over. Amanda was glad that things were peaceful again.

"How did your first day of school go, Amanda?" Mother asked.

"Fine."

"Pearly didn't bother you?"

"No."

"Good," Mother said. "Are you very far behind?"

"I don't think so," Amanda said.

"What you don't realize, Mother, is that Amanda's the smart kid in this family," Dale said. "She doesn't have to work hard to get decent marks like me. It comes naturally to her."

"Don't be foolish, Dale. It comes naturally to you too. You're just modest." Mother reached out fondly and tousled his hair. "Gorgeous, modest and a great athlete. When's your first game?"

"Saturday," he said, without much enthusiasm.

"Good, you can expect your regular rooters to be there," Mother said.

"I may skip it myself," Dale said.

"Skip it? You're not serious," Mother said. "If you want to win an athletic scholarship—"

"Mother," Dale interrupted. "I was talking to my coach, and he says the colleges aren't looking for supporting players like me. They're after the stars. He doesn't think I have a chance."

The silence was ominous. Mother's expression didn't change, but when she finally spoke, her voice quavered.

"Of course you're going to win some kind of scholarship, Dale. Perhaps not athletic, but—The cost of an Ivy League school is just prohibitive unless one—Of *course,* you'll win something."

"Don't count on me even getting into an Ivy League school," Dale said gloomily.

As soon as they'd entered the house, Amanda had returned Pink Pig to the miniature shelf to enjoy a well-deserved snooze in the sun. When bedtime came, and Amanda took her friend down to say good night, Pink Pig was trembling. "What's wrong?" Amanda asked. "Are you sick?"

"Scared," Pink Pig said. "The mists around Wizard's castle are gone. All gone. That means trouble is coming to the Little World."

"What kind of trouble?" Amanda asked.

"It depends on what he sees that he doesn't like, but he's sure to find something he doesn't like, and then he'll change it. Wizard is powerful enough to change anything in the Little World."

"More powerful than you, Pink Pig?"

"Me? I have no power at all, except as your friend."

"Maybe nothing will happen," Amanda said. "The Little World is so nice. Maybe Wizard will like the way it is."

"I hope so," Pink Pig said, but her black-speck eyes still glistened with fear.

Three

Amanda reminded Mother about Back-to-School Night as soon as they sat down to supper. "Tonight?" Mother said. "Oh, darling, you should have told me about it sooner."

"I did," Amanda said. "I gave you the notice Monday."

"But the coach is letting Dale play right wing in the soccer game tonight, sweetheart. This is Dale's big chance. We want to see him win, don't we?"

Before Amanda could answer, Dale said, "Come on, Mother, you're making too big a deal of it. I'm not likely to do anything special and Manda only has one Back-to-School Night a year."

"Amanda's never cared whether I went or not, and even so I haven't missed one yet. You never have cared, have you?" Mother demanded.

Amanda shook her head mutely. It was true Back-to-

School Night had never mattered to her, but this one was different.

"Suppose you *do* do something spectacular, Dale," Mother said, "after all my years of faithful attendance, I deserve to witness it, don't I?"

"I wish you'd get it through your head that your son is just an average student and an ordinary athlete, not a hotshot."

"Don't you want me at your game, Dale?" Mother was looking at him with tears in her eyes.

Dale relented. "Sure, I want you. Hey, I know you're always out there rooting for me and I appreciate it. Really, I do." He shrugged. "What do you say, Manda?"

She knew he wanted her to stand up for herself. Timidly she told her mother, "Mr. Whittier said he wants to meet you. And Vera's mother is coming."

"I'm sure I can meet them both some other time," Mother said. She sounded cheerful again. "Tell you what, Manda. You can invite Vera for a sleep-over. You'd like that, wouldn't you?"

"I thought we were going to Vermont to check out Middlebury College this weekend," Dale said.

"Vera doesn't have to come any particular weekend. Next one will do just as well. Right, Amanda?"

Amanda nodded.

"Lovely," Mother said to her. "Now I leave it to you. Shall we go to Dale's soccer game or to your Back-to-School Night?" Mother's bright smile pretended she didn't really care which Amanda chose, but Amanda knew better.

"The game," Amanda said. Disappointment made a small puddle in her stomach. Mr. Whittier had said he wanted to tell her Mother how impressed he was that Amanda had caught up with her class so quickly. Also her latest Pink Pig story, marked A+, was hanging on Ms. Hart's bulletin board. Next year she wasn't likely to have plusses like that to show Mother. Dutifully, Amanda got up to help Dale do the dishes.

Even in jeans and a heavy sweater Mother appeared dressed-up compared to the other people watching the soccer game that evening. The way she held her head made people look at her as if she were a celebrity. Several times Mother stopped to greet people and ask how they were. She kissed cheeks with a woman Amanda didn't know and laughed away a compliment from the heavyset man who'd sold her her car. Playing the charmer, Dale called it. "How's this, Amanda?" Mother asked about seats in the third row of the stands.

Amanda couldn't see over the heads of the adults in front of her, but she was just as glad. She didn't mind watching when Dale was being a fullback in soccer or a forward in basketball, which he played in the winter. Then he wasn't doing any of the actual scoring in games, just running and fending off balls, if it was soccer, or dribbling them down the court and handing them off to other players, if it was basketball. But tonight the coach had given Dale a chance to show what a good corner kicker he was. As right wing, the pressure was on him to score for the team, and that made Amanda too anxious to watch him. If he did something wonderful, then she would share in the after-game high. Meanwhile, Amanda had another concern.

As soon as everyone around her got absorbed in the game, Amanda took Pink Pig out of her pocket. In the blink of an instant, Pink Pig changed from glassy quartz to soft live flesh. Amanda leaned her elbows on her knees and held Pink Pig cupped close to her lips so that they could talk unobserved.

"I'm so glad you've come," Pink Pig said, as anxious-sounding as Amanda had ever heard her.

"What's happened?"

"Trouble, terrible trouble," Pink Pig said. "The circus people were rehearsing in the village square and Wizard sent his dragon roaring down the hill to breathe fire at them. They all ran into the woods and are afraid to come out of hiding. Frog says Wizard hates freaks. Besides, you know how tall Spangled Giraffe and Brass Elephant are? Well, they peered into his castle windows out of curiosity. Clown was with them, but Ballerina wasn't and she's had to run away too."

"That's terrible, Pink Pig." Amanda was shocked to hear that the peace of the Little World was shattered. "How long will they have to stay away?"

"I don't know. I can't remember a time when the veils of mist ever disappeared from Wizard's castle. Wizard has always done his magic in there, guarded by his two knights and his dragon. He's never bothered us much. Even when he rides through the Little World in his gold and red coach, we don't see him because he makes himself invisible."

"Somebody must know what to do about him," Amanda said.

"Frog might. He's wise. But it's a long journey to his pond."

"We'll have to go anyway," Amanda said.

A roar went up from the people in the seats around

41

her, and Amanda glanced at Mother, who was clapping her long, thin fingers together in excitement at something that had happened on the field. The adults around Amanda jumped to their feet. Dale's team had just scored a goal. Amanda stood up too, but a picket fence of bodies in front of her kept her from seeing the players.

"I can't go now. Is it safe to wait?" Amanda whispered to Pink Pig.

"I'm not going without you," Pink Pig said. "We'll wait."

A few minutes later the crowd subsided and sat back down. Not long after, the game ended.

"Well, it was worth watching, wasn't it?" Mother asked Amanda. Mother's cheeks were pink from the cool fall evening and her blue eyes sparkled. "It was such a thrill to see Dale boot in that goal. Too bad his team didn't win. We'll wait outside the locker room for him."

Other people were waiting in the hall of the high school outside the gym—team members' girlfriends, fathers, mothers, sisters, younger brothers. Amanda saw the redheaded girl who had once been Dale's girlfriend, his secret girlfriend. He'd told Amanda, but never Mother. Eventually he'd said, "She's not my girl anymore, Manda. Just holding hands in the hall wasn't her idea of a satisfactory relationship." He'd shaken his head and said, as if it puzzled him, "She wanted me to make more time in my life for her, but where did she expect me to get it from?"

"Sports?" Amanda had said.

"Who would I be then? And I sure can't afford to study less. Maybe Mother's right. She says having a girlfriend in high school, when you're not in control of your impulses yet, is bad news. She met Dad in high school . . . I guess marrying him was the worst mistake of her life."

"Why? Was he bad?"

"Not bad, just wrong for her. He did yard work for Mother's father. All the other guys were scared stiff of Mother's father—he was a writer, like of biographies—but Dad stood up to the old man even when Mother's father was mean drunk. So Mother thought Roland Bickett was a hero. That was before she met Pearly."

A woman who was also waiting outside the gym was talking at Mother. Amanda could tell by Mother's polite smile that she'd rather not be listening. "I told Bobby he can make all the goals he wants; what's really going to count are those SAT scores," the woman said. "But get that kid to study—fat chance!"

"One would hope the admissions people look at the whole boy and not just his SAT scores," Mother said.

"Depends on the school. Bobby's got an edge, of course, because his father went to Yale, and they'll take that into account . . . Where's Dale applying?"

"Oh, Princeton, and some of the better smaller schools that have excellent teacher-student ratios," Mother said.

"Dale's that good a student?" The woman sounded surprised.

"He's an unusual boy," Mother said. "I'm sure they'll take that into account, as well as where his father went to school." She smiled her toothpaste-ad smile at the woman and turned to Amanda. "Are you sleepy, darling? Our soccer star deserves an ice cream treat after his performance, don't you think?"

43

Amanda nodded. Mother started fussing with Amanda's hair, and the woman she'd been talking to gave up and moved away.

Dale came out finally. Two of his teammates were walking with him. Baby-faced Denny was saying to him, "I'm telling you, Dale, she'll give in if you ask her. You've got a way with teachers."

"It's your good-guy image, kid," the long-nosed fellow on the other side of Dale said. "Or maybe you're the only one of us who looks like your socks don't smell."

"What are they trying to talk you into, darling?" Mother asked smiling. All three boys looked startled, as if they hadn't noticed her before.

"We need a favor from a hard-nosed teacher, Mrs. Bickett, and your son's the one to charm her into it," Denny said.

"Mother, Amanda, you know Denny and Mike?" After Dale had introduced them, Mother made a comment about what a good game they had all played.

"Yeah, if Dale can get us sprung from school earlier, we might have a better chance of winning the next one," Mike, the long-nosed one, said. "Well, you coming to the party later, Dale?"

"If I can get a ride," Dale said.

"Yikes, there's mine. See you." Denny abruptly took off for the parking lot as a car honked and began pulling away from the building.

"Hey, that's my ride too!" Mike said, and ran after Denny.

"Dale," Mother said when they were alone, "you didn't mention any party. I thought you planned some late-night study for that test you said was so important tomorrow morning."

"Well, yeah." He looked uncomfortable.

"We could stop in for ice cream and you'd still have enough time," Mother said.

"All right, and then maybe you could drop me at the party? I can get a ride home after, no sweat."

"You're going to skip the studying?"

Dale sighed. "I'm a little sick of it, Mother. It's not getting me anywhere, and this is my senior year. Colleges look mostly at your earlier record."

"But your earlier record isn't exactly outstanding," Mother said. "Don't slack off now, Dale." Her voice shook with emotion. "This is the most crucial time in your life. You *have* to make it into the right school, or . . . My father used to say that if he had only gone to the right school, his whole life would have been different. Please believe me, darling. You mustn't let up now."

He looked unhappy, but he smiled anyway and said, "Okay, calm down. We'll have some ice cream and I'll go hit the books. I guess missing one more party won't kill me."

"Oh, darling," Mother said with feeling, "I don't want you to miss *any* parties. I don't want you to miss out on anything in life."

"I know, I know." He hugged her. Mother took his arm. Amanda walked beside him on the other side. She shivered in the chill wind that had come up. "Cold?" he asked Amanda quietly.

"I'm glad you were so good," she said.

"Yeah, too bad I wasn't good enough to make a dif-

45

ference, but thanks." He gave her an affectionate squeeze.

It was late and Amanda was very sleepy when they got home. She took Pink Pig into bed with her, but despite the urgency of consulting Frog, Amanda fell asleep before they could start on the journey.

Amanda carried her tray with soup, a frankfurter and a container of milk to the table near the window where Vera and Libby were saving a seat for her. "You didn't get dessert today," Vera said.

"I don't like Jell-O," Amanda told her, "and the white cake's always dry."

"I don't see how you can eat so much and stay so skinny," Vera said. "If I ate as much as you, I'd weigh a ton."

"Amanda's lucky. Her whole family's thin," Libby said. "And you should see her brother! He's gorgeous."

"Bickett," Vera said. "Was that his picture in the paper this morning with the soccer team?"

Amanded nodded.

Libby said, "Yes, and he plays basketball and runs track too. He's really something."

"Is he nice to you?" Vera asked.

"Uh huh," Amanda said.

"*My* brother's a pig," Vera said. "You should see the way he leaves the bathroom, and guess who gets to use it first? I can't stand my brother. I can't wait until he goes off to college."

"I like my brothers," Libby said. "One of them's always around to drive me to the mall when I want to go, and I get the most allowance in my family because my brothers pay me to do their chores sometimes."

"Did you buy the makeup kit yet?" Amanda asked.

"Manda, can't you see I'm wearing eye shadow?" Libby said. She closed her eyes obligingly so that Amanda could see.

"Oh, yes. It looks interesting." Libby's eyes were set deep above her plump cheeks and the eye shadow was barely visible. Just as well, Amanda thought; makeup looked peculiar on fifth graders.

"Bickett," Vera said again. "That lady janitor's name is Bickett too. Is she a relative of yours, Amanda?"

"Um hmm." Amanda had a mouthful of frankfurter.

"She is?" Libby sounded astonished. "What's she to you, Amanda?"

Amanda swallowed and said, "Grandmother."

"You're kidding!" Libby looked surprised. "Your mother looks so expensive. Is Pearly her mother or your father's?"

"My father's," Amanda said, and added, "We don't have anything to do with her."

"Why not?" Vera asked.

"I think because my father left us right after I was born," Amanda said uncertainly.

"Pearly Bickett is Amanda's grandmother," Vera said with relish. "Now how about that!"

"Pearly's a nice lady," Libby said.

"She's a character," Vera said. "My father says Pearly thinks *she* runs this school."

"Well, she really can make kids behave," Libby said.

"You think she's nice?" Amanda asked Libby.

47

"Sure. She used to lend my brother lunch money when he didn't have any. Besides I think she's funny the way she calls everybody 'angel.'"

"What does she talk about to you, Amanda?" Vera asked.

"Nothing. I'm not even sure she knows who I am."

"You ought to say hello to her and tell her," Vera said.

"Why?"

"Because. Aren't you interested in getting to know your own grandmother?"

Amanda didn't answer. Despite what Libby said, Amanda didn't know if Pearly was nice, and anyway, Mother wouldn't like it if Amanda had anything to do with her grandmother.

Pearly was mopping up a mess in front of the wall of lockers when Amanda and Libby and Vera walked down the hall toward art, which was the period after lunch that day. Vera stopped short.

"Hi, Pearly," Vera said.

"Hi, angel. How are you?"

"I'm fine. I wanted to introduce you to somebody you ought to know."

Amanda's heart tripped in surprise at Vera's boldness.

"This is Amanda Bickett. She's your granddaughter," Vera said.

Pearly's face changed. Her brown eyes saddened and her smile drooped. She looked right at Amanda and said, "I know who Amanda is." Then she seemed to pull herself up and with her usual cheerful energy, she asked, "Well, did you girls have a good lunch today? I could smell those franks and that sauerkraut way out here. Any of you have a frankfurter?"

"Me," Amanda whispered.

"With sauerkraut?"

"Plain," Amanda said.

"Not even no mustard? Isn't that something! Me, I love it with everything on. Rather eat franks than anything." She took a breath, and when no one spoke or made a move to leave, she took hold of the conversation again. ". . . Kid dropped his science experiment out here. That's what I'm cleaning up. Just dropped it and walked off. I guess his Mama cleans up after him at home."

"We're going to be late," Libby whispered.

"Better get to class," Pearly said, beaming at them all. "Have a good afternoon now."

"You too, Pearly," Vera said.

"See," Libby said as they sat down in a row in the classroom, with Libby in the middle. "Isn't she nice?"

"I guess so," Amanda said.

The last bell finally rang and Amanda rushed down the hall with everybody else hurrying to get on the buses for home. Pearly was cleaning the glass display case near the stairway close to the front doors. "Amanda," Pearly called.

Amanda stopped and tensed. "Yes?"

"Come here so I can say something to you," Pearly said, and when Amanda crept close, Pearly lowered her voice and said quietly, "I didn't want you to think I'd ignore my own grandchild. I knew who you was all right, but I didn't want to push in on you. When your brother was in this school, I told him any time he needed help, I was here. The same thing goes for you. I'm not going to bother you none, but if you need me, I'm here."

"Thank you," Amanda said. She looked up into eyes that were brimfull of tenderness. "Thank you," she said again, and ran for the bus.

49

Four

As soon as she was home alone, Amanda rushed into the Little World with Pink Pig. "The circus people and Ballerina are still hiding. Everything's too quiet. We better get to Frog quickly now," Pink Pig said.

Looking at the castle which rose like a gray stone vulture on its hill above the village, Amanda shuddered and agreed. They left Peasant Woman sitting with a black shawl over her long woolen dress, calmly shelling peas on the bench outside her cottage. They passed Peasant Man bent like a black question mark as he hoed his garden. He was too deaf to hear Amanda calling hello to him.

The brown dirt road was soft under Amanda's feet as she and Pink Pig walked by empty fields full of daisies and goldenrod and flowing grasses.

"Look at all the birds flying about," Pink Pig said. "I've never seen so many in the air all at once."

Amanda looked up. Ordinarily in the Little World, an exotic bird might be flying by or perched on a low tree branch. It would be preening its black-speckled red feathers, or tossing the orange cockade on its head, or flapping great pink and green wings. Today Amanda counted nine varicolored birds circling overhead.

"Oh, no!" Pink Pig said, and began trotting as fast as her short legs would carry her toward the deep woods. Amanda ran too although she couldn't see anything but that the woods had a strangely metallic glow to them.

"That explains it. The birds don't know where to alight," Pink Pig said when they'd arrived at the woods. "Wizard has changed their trees to metal."

Amanda stood puffing beside Pink Pig, staring at the strange gold-colored shapes that looked more like a sculptor's vision than like real trees. The metallic shapes reflected the sun with an unpleasant glare. "Those poor birds can't nest in metal trees," Amanda said.

"And what about the insects and the other creatures that feed in the woods? Think of the deer and the rabbits. Oh, imagine the poor rabbits!" Pink Pig sounded ready to cry.

"What makes Wizard so mean?" Amanda asked.

"Frog says Wizard just likes to change things and doesn't care if his changes cause trouble. He could destroy the Little World with his magic experiments now that he's doing them outside his castle."

"Someone must talk to him," Amanda said. "Could Peasant Man and Peasant Woman go to Wizard and beg him to bring the woods back to life?"

"Peasant Man and Peasant Woman accept whatever

51

happens. They don't try to change what is. Besides, you know they don't have the power of speech."

To Amanda, one of the most curious things in the Little World was that some inhabitants who looked human, like Peasant Man and Peasant Woman, Peasant Girl, and Ballerina, couldn't speak, while others who looked animal, like Pink Pig and Frog, spoke and thought as well as Amanda did. "Do you think Wizard would listen if you went to him?" Amanda asked.

"Me?" Pink Pig squealed. "Not me. I'm afraid of Wizard."

"He's not evil, is he?"

"He can be." Then Pink Pig thought and added, "But if he wants to, he can make good changes. Once Wild Horse lay in a ditch suffering from a broken leg. When Wizard rode by in his coach, he pointed his crooked finger and Wild Horse jumped up good as new."

"Well, if Wizard isn't altogether evil, and someone made him understand the damage he's done here, maybe he'd undo it."

Pink Pig wrinkled her snout and her tiny black eyes worried at Amanda. "I don't know anyone brave enough to approach Wizard."

The road did seem endless as they followed its curve toward the far distant point where it disappeared. Amanda got tired and complained, "I don't understand what good it is for Frog to know so much if he never leaves his pond and only catches flies and swims."

"Things don't always have a use in the Little World," Pink Pig said. "Some just *are* without a reason. Does that bother you a lot?"

"Yes," Amanda said. "I like things to make sense."

She thought of her mother, whose wishes sometimes didn't make sense. The truth was that things didn't always have a use or a reason in her world either.

They passed deep green woods still untouched by Wizard, and were surprised to find Peasant Girl walking toward them this far from the village. She carried the flowers she'd collected in a basket on each plump arm. Amanda and Pink Pig walked by a lake on which two sailboats drifted, one transparent as glass and the other gray as pewter. A mallard duck with a glossy green head paddled in the shallows.

"It's so beautiful here and everybody seems content," Amanda said. "Why couldn't all the creatures band together to fight Wizard?"

"But he has two knights to defend him," Pink Pig said. "Not to mention the dragon. And Wild Horse is his friend ever since Wizard saved him from the ditch. Besides, Wizard has magic. We could never win by fighting."

"Could we talk the knights into rebelling? They must see that Wizard is harming the Little World."

"Those knights aren't thinking creatures, just doers like Ballerina and Cat with the Ball of Yarn. We don't have many thinkers in the Little World."

"*You* think, Pink Pig," Amanda said.

"Not more than I have to. Thinking is hard," Pink Pig replied. "I'm only a pig, good for snoozing in the sun or keeping you company."

To the left of the road was a black pond full of floating lily pads. "Here's Frog's pond at last," Pink Pig said.

Amanda saw big-eyed, green Frog next to a cup-shaped white lily. He was reclining on his side, holding up his large head with one limb. He did look smart.

53

"Good afternoon, Frog," Pink Pig said. "Did you know that the veils of mist have gone from Wizard's castle?"

"Have you not come to call because I know it all?" Frog asked. His long tongue unfurled and flipped a fly back into his mouth.

"Then you know what to do about Wizard?" Pink Pig asked.

"The right question from you should not be what but who," Frog said, and yawned.

"Excuse me," Pink Pig said. "I don't understand you." She looked at Amanda. "Do you understand him?"

"Who then?" Amanda asked Frog.

"Pink Pig and you, you two are who."

"But how can *we* do anything?" Pink Pig asked. "She's only a child in her world, and I'm just a pig in this one. We're not strong enough. Not brave enough either. At least I'm not."

"The trouble here is grave. You really must be brave," Frog said. "You both know how to talk and also how to walk. That's most of what you need to accomplish the deed."

"You mean we should talk to Wizard?" Amanda asked. "But why would he listen to us?"

"Your power is much. You know how to touch. More I cannot say. Good-bye for today." He hopped off the pad and his bumpy green body disappeared in the black water of the pond.

"What could he mean, that we know how to touch Wizard?" Amanda asked Pink Pig. "Do you think he meant with our hands? Or . . ." She thought of other ways of touching—with words, with feelings, with a look, the way Pearly had touched her in the hallway on the way out of school.

54

"Even if we could figure that out," Pink Pig said, looking very discouraged, "we still have a problem. I'm not brave. Can you be?"

"I don't know," Amanda said. "But I'm willing to try."

Pink Pig's black-speck eyes glistened with admiration as she looked up at Amanda. "As Frog would put it," Pink Pig said, "if you must try, then so must I."

It had been Vera's idea that the three of them should have a pajama party and also her idea that Libby's house would be the most fun because of all her older brothers.

"My mother says we can't," Libby reported next day.

"Can't why?" Vera asked.

Libby looked embarrassed and answered vaguely, "I guess she's too busy."

"I'll ask my mother," Amanda said, to rescue Libby from the questions with which Vera was sure to pepper her. Libby had confided to Amanda that her mother didn't like children. She didn't mind being pregnant, or taking care of babies, but after that she lost interest in raising them. Libby's mother said pregnancy was a blissful state, even nicer than being alone with her potter's wheel, but her pots were easier to mold and shape than a child. Libby claimed her father did whatever mothering was done at their house. Except that since he'd become unemployed, he was too depressed to do much either.

"Why don't we go to your house?" Libby asked Vera.

"Mine's no good because of my hateful horrible brother. We'll go to your house then, Amanda," Vera decided.

Mother seemed so surprised that Amanda wanted to invite friends for a sleep-over that Amanda reminded her it had been her suggestion originally. "I've never had a sleep-over with friends," Amanda said.

"No, you haven't," Mother said then, "and it's time you did." She kissed Amanda's forehead, and added, "I'm glad you're developing some social interests, Amanda. It's always worried me that you're so self-contained. I'd like it if you learned to talk to people. Who knows, you might even start talking to me."

"I do talk to you," Amanda protested.

"Maybe you do—as much as you can. Dale's being such a chatterbox as a little boy spoiled me, I suppose . . . Anyway, a sleep-over's a good idea."

Mother walked away leaving Amanda feeling as if a bee had stung her.

At the last minute Libby had to go to the wedding of a distant cousin which her mother had forgotten to tell her about. Amanda didn't look forward to a weekend alone with Vera. Even for short periods of time it was a struggle to like her, although Amanda kept trying for Libby's sake.

Friday evening promptly at eight, the doorbell chimed. Mother stood behind Amanda who opened the door. The principal's wife sat in her car at the curb waiting for her daughter to be received. "If Vera gets too obnoxious, just ship her home," the principal's wife called out. "We'll be gone, but her big brother'll be there."

"Oh, I'm sure we'll have a lovely time together," Mother said.

56

"Good luck," the principal's wife said and waved as she zoomed off.

Vera stepped into the living room leaning back against the weight of the overnight bag which she was holding with both hands. "Oh, what a cute little place! Just like a doll's house." She looked around. "Everything's so pretty. Like out of a magazine." Still carrying the case she stepped over to the wall on which Mother's lock collection was displayed. "What are all these things?"

The first hour passed easily. Vera put down her case as Mother explained how the ingenious locks worked and where the ornamental locks had come from. Amanda sat waiting patiently. ". . . And this is a fish lock," Mother said of the last one on the wall. "It comes from the Orient and was used on a jewelry chest. See how cleverly it works? . . . If you like handiwork, I'll show you the embroidered bellpulls in my bedroom. I found the most incredibly detailed one done in silk tucked away in a corner of an antique shop . . ."

Amanda yawned. She wished she could read her library book until Mother and Vera got tired of each other, but it wouldn't be polite. "You have such good taste, Mrs. Bickett," Vera was saying. "I wish my mother did. All she cares about is food. She's a dietician. Also exercise. She's always trying to make me eat straw and shape up. Do you exercise?"

"Only when I have to," Mother said.

"I knew it, and look how svelte you are! My mother thinks you can pound yourself into svelteness, but frankly I think it's a lost cause when you start out square like my mother and me."

57

"But you can always do something with what you have," Mother said, and she talked to Vera earnestly about straight lines and what a lovely nose Vera had. "Colors are important," Mother said. She and Vera disappeared into Mother's bedroom to see what Vera's best colors were. Since Amanda hadn't been invited, she thought it was all right to get her book and read now. Eventually, Vera reappeared alone and asked Amanda what they were going to do next.

"I don't know," Amanda said. "What would you like to do?"

"Why don't you show me your miniatures? Your mother says you collect them."

Obediently Amanda led the way behind the curtain into her bedroom area. "Your mother's so beautiful and so nice," Vera said wistfully. "I wish my mother were like her. You're so lucky, Amanda." Vera looked around the six by ten feet of Amanda's space, most of which was taken up with a canopied bed with a dust ruffle. "But you sure have a tiny bedroom."

Vera wasn't very interested in Amanda's miniatures. Probably had enough of looking at other people's things, Amanda thought. They sat down on the bed and tried without success to decide on something to do.

"Does your brother look like your mother or like you?"

"Like her," Amanda said.

"I bet you look like your father. Did you say he's dead?"

"He died, but that was a long time after he left us. Anyway, I don't know what he looked like."

"You ought to ask Pearly about him. Does your mother hate him too much to tell you about him?"

Amanda didn't say anything. She didn't know how else to get out of answering Vera's bold questions. It would be rude to tell Vera it was none of her business, even though that's what Amanda thought. Mother was still bitter about how Roland Bickett had gone to the supermarket to buy a box of diapers for his newborn daughter and never come back. "He was a totally irresponsible man," Mother had said. And when Amanda had asked if he was nice before he ran away, Mother got so red with anger that Amanda had been afraid. "How can you ask me a question like that?" Mother had said, and then, as if she'd forgotten it was she who had brought up the subject, she had said, "Don't ever mention him to me again."

"Don't you have any stuffed animals?" Vera was asking. "I have dozens, and I have a dollhouse too with Victorian furniture . . . I bet I have more books than you do. My father's always giving me books. He gets a lot of them from school, of course, and then he gets an educator's discount. I like biographies best. How about you?"

"I like fairy tales and books like *The Lion, the Witch and the Wardrobe*," Amanda said.

"Let's go in the living room and play a game," Vera said. "Your bedroom gives me claustrophobia. What games do you have?"

"I have Chinese checkers and cards," Amanda said.

"No electronic games? I bet your brother has some. Mine has lots."

"I don't touch my brother's things," Amanda said. "We could play Go Fish or rummy."

"Yuck," Vera said. "Let's go see what your mother is doing."

59

Dutifully Amanda followed her guest through the living room to the kitchen where Mother had spread out her manicuring set and was doing her nails. She had long, shapely nails that she carefully repolished twice a week. "Mind if we watch?" Vera asked, and settled herself with her elbows on the table when Mother smiled and said she didn't mind at all.

"My mother's nails are always splitting. Yours are just beautiful," Vera said.

A while later Mother was lacquering the nails on Vera's pale bumpy fingers while Amanda sat silently listening to the easy flow of chatter between them.

"I can't believe that you're related to Pearly," Vera was saying. "Of course, it was only by marriage, but still—she's so plain and ordinary and you're so elegant. Her son mustn't have been at all like her."

Amanda held her breath. Vera had barged into sacred territory. However, Mother didn't get angry. All she said was, "He disguised himself in a military uniform shortly after I met him. I thought he was dashing and strong and certain to rise to high places."

"And did he?"

"No."

"Was he mean to you?" Vera asked.

"No, he wasn't a mean person, just not the right person for me. A girl should never marry in her teens. It takes time to get rid of your romantic illusions and discover what's really important in life."

"What's really important?" Vera asked, wide-eyed.

"Why, a person's upbringing, their culture, their education."

"Not how good-looking they are, you mean?" Vera said.

"Well, appearance matters too," Mother cautioned.

Amanda stopped listening. She thought about what she knew of her parents' life together, how Mother had disliked trailing after her husband from one dreary army post to another while she struggled to raise Dale and collect enough credits for a college degree in business. She'd finally stayed put in Houston, Texas, when she got the degree and a job, and let Roland Bickett move on without her, but he'd returned after a few years of separation. Then they moved back to their home town. Amanda was born, and he went out for that box of diapers and never came back. Even if her husband wasn't good enough for her, as Dale had said, Mother must have liked him a lot if she'd tried to live with him a second time.

Roland, Amanda thought. What would a person named Roland be like? She'd never thought of her father as a person. There were no pictures or letters to construct him from. Amanda imagined someone colorless and thin in an army uniform and put a smile on his face. But he had left after she was born—because she was born?

"You know," Mother was saying to Vera, "I'm sure you're going to be good for Amanda. You're a mature, perceptive girl, and she's so shy and undeveloped."

"Well, I'll try," Vera said.

Dale walked into the kitchen then. "Am I barging into an all-girl party?" he asked.

"You're welcome, darling," Mother said and intro-

61

duced him to Vera, who gawked at him open-mouthed. For once she had no question or comment. Mother asked him if he'd enjoyed the meeting he'd gone to.

"It was okay," Dale said. "But all they had to eat was pretzels and potato chips. Do we have any real food around?" He opened the refrigerator and took out a wedge of cheese. "Carrot sticks, carrot sticks, carrot sticks. It's no wonder everyone in this family is thin."

"There's a chocolate cake behind the salad bowl," Mother said triumphantly. "I thought the girls would like a midnight snack."

"I love chocolate," Vera said.

"Thank you, Mother," Amanda said softly, pleased that for her sake Mother had thought to stop at a bakery on her way home from work.

"There, you *can* talk," Mother said as Dale took out the cake and began cutting slices for everybody. "Amanda has left all the gossiping to Vera and me," she told Dale.

"Maybe she likes her own world better," Dale said.

"What do you mean, her own world?" Vera asked.

"Amanda's got a fantasy world where she spends most of her time," Dale said. "My little sister has a great imagination."

"Which you had something to do with," Mother said to Dale with a smile. "The things you used to have her believing when she was little!"

"What things?" Vera asked.

"All I remember is telling her she had a fairy godmother. How old were you when you stopped believing that one, Manda?" he asked.

Amanda stood up abruptly, and, ignoring her mother's voice calling her back, escaped to her room. If she'd had a door, she would have locked herself in. It was bad enough that her mother thought Vera was better than she, but to have Dale betray her! How could he have talked about her like that to Vera, whom he didn't even know? When Amanda had confided her adventures in the Little World and her friendship with Pink Pig to him years ago, he had listened and said solemnly, "I'm glad you have a good friend, Amanda. I wish I did."

Together they had puzzled over the mystery of who sent the miniatures in their plain-brown-bag wrapping every year. And it was a mystery. Even now it was.

"Do you think my father sends them?" she had asked Dale when she had pulled out the beautiful green-headed miniature ceramic mallard duck from the shredded paper along with the usual hand-printed unsigned note that said, "For a dear little girl." It was the year before Mother told them their father had died.

"Not him. He's not the type, Amanda."

"What type is he?"

"The type that stuck Mother with two kids to raise. A bad-news character, a deadbeat."

"But how do you know?"

"He lived with us a year before you were born," Dale said. "I remember him. Don't think I don't. Don't think about him, Manda. You must have a fairy godmother who remembers your birthday."

She had thought it might be Dale himself, but then she had discovered that each year on his birthday he got an unmarked envelope with a bill inside and an unsigned card saying, "For a good boy."

"We both have a fairy godmother," she'd said to him.

"No," he'd said. "All I have is Mother."

Amanda had always accepted that Mother loved Dale best. It was natural that she would. Dale was so good and loving and handsome, and besides, he could make Mother happy. Being loved second-best wasn't so bad, especially since Amanda had a kind and understanding brother. Also, she had a fairy godmother somewhere. Pink Pig had assured her she did.

Alone in her room, Amanda took Pink Pig down from her station and asked her, "Why did they talk that way to Vera about me? Don't they understand anything?" With her eyes squeezed shut, she held Pink Pig tight against her cheek.

"Who are you talking to?" Vera wanted to know. She'd walked into Amanda's bedroom uninvited. It was, after all, her bedroom too for the weekend, Amanda reminded herself.

"Just—nobody."

"I hope you don't mind my saying this, Amanda," Vera said, "but you're a little strange."

"Why?"

"Well, I never met anybody as quiet as you. I thought you were just shy, but I've been here a whole evening already and you haven't said three words to me."

"What do you want to talk about?"

Vera plunked down on the end of the bed. "Tell me about your brother. He's gorgeous. He looks just like your mother and she's the most beautiful woman I've ever met. Does he have a lot of girlfriends?"

"No."

"Well, what's he like?"

"He's nice . . . He does sports. He's on the soccer team and the basketball team and in the spring he runs."

"And he doesn't tease you or make you do his jobs or anything?"

"No."

"You're so lucky. Does he have a lot of friends?"

"I think so."

"What do you mean, you think so? Doesn't he bring them home?"

"No."

"Amanda," Vera said impatiently, "can't you answer more than yes or no? We're not playing Twenty Questions."

Amanda got angry. She said, "I'm glad you like my brother, but you sound as if you don't like me much, and I don't want to answer your questions."

Vera looked surprised. "Well!" she said. "I guess you're not such a wimp as I thought. Okay, I'm sorry. But you do drive me crazy being so mysterious. What do you have to hide?"

Amanda kept her temper and reminded herself that Vera was her guest. "We should get ready for bed," Amanda said. "Do you want to use the bathroom first?"

Vera shrugged. "You go first. I can wait."

Amanda took her flannel nightgown with the frill around the neck into the bathroom. She showered quickly, brushed her teeth and came out ready for bed. Vera was sitting cross-legged on the living room floor talking to Dale, who was watching the eleven-o'clock news with Mother. He was lying at Mother's feet with his head on a cushion.

"Would you like your cake before you go to bed?" Mother asked when she saw Amanda.

"No, thank you." Amanda waited, but seeing that

65

Vera had no intention of moving, she said, "Good night, everybody."

"Don't I get a kiss?" Mother asked, as if that was their nightly ritual. She held out her arms gracefully and Amanda moved to kiss her. Vera was watching enviously. Amanda could have told her that Mother was only playacting for Vera's benefit, but Amanda didn't tell on people.

She lay in bed listening to their voices. The eleven-o'clock news was over, but they were all still talking and laughing. If Libby were here, it wouldn't be like this. Libby was *her* friend. She'd be whispering in bed beside Amanda, sharing secrets. Amanda heard her own name and squeezed the pillow over her ear so as not to know what they were saying about her. She lay against the far edge of the bed, leaving most of it free for Vera who would have to come to sleep sometime. Pink Pig wriggled sympathetically in Amanda's grasp, her tiny hooves pressing against Amanda's palm.

"You don't have to invite her ever again," Pink Pig said.

"I don't like her."

"Tell Libby."

"Then Libby would have to choose."

"She'd choose you."

"But suppose she didn't?"

"You're scared?"

"A little."

Pink Pig sighed. "I thought you were going to be so brave," she said. "I thought you were going to be brave enough to face Wizard."

66

"That's different," Amanda said. "I could be that kind of brave maybe, but I can't risk losing my friend."

"Will we do it soon?" Pink Pig asked.

"Soon," Amanda promised.

It was then she heard the pounding hoofbeats of oncoming horses. At first she thought it was her own heart beating fast. Then she realized she was standing beside Pink Pig a few feet from the road, and Wizard was coming in his gold and red coach, coming right toward her. She wanted to run, but she didn't. Pink Pig squealed in terror. The dark horses drew abreast and stopped. Amanda looked into the coach. No one sat on the velvet cushions. The coach was empty. For an anxious bit of time, the coach stood there. Then the horses reared and plunged into motion and the coach disappeared down the road toward the village.

"He saw us. He looked at us. Oh, Amanda, what's going to happen now?"

"How do you know he was in the coach?" Amanda asked.

"He was. I told you he can make himself invisible," Pink Pig said. "I could feel him, and he was angry."

"But we haven't done anything yet. So he can't be angry with us," Amanda said. "Next time I'm going to say something to him."

"What?"

"I don't know. It's hard to talk to someone who's invisible. But I will."

"Yes," Pink Pig said. "Next time you'll be brave. But I hope you're right that he wasn't angry with us." She sounded worried. Amanda was worried too, about whether she would be brave. Next time.

Five

Somehow, Amanda thought, spending the weekend together had made a difference in the way Vera treated her. She didn't like the difference. "Hurry up, Manda," Vera said, and took Amanda's arm to hustle her into homeroom as if she were a not very bright child in Vera's charge.

Vera perked up when she saw Libby already sitting there. "Manda and I had such a fun weekend," Vera said to Libby. "Too bad you missed it." Then without asking how Libby had enjoyed the wedding, Vera gushed, "Her brother's a dream. He's just as gorgeous as Manda's mother. She took us to the mall and had her face made up by the demonstration lady. She said we could each buy some blusher, but Manda wanted a book instead."

While Vera was catching her breath, Amanda asked quickly, "How was your weekend, Libby?"

"Okay." Libby sounded suspiciously unenthusiastic.

"Then we watched Dale play soccer," Vera continued, "and we could have played tennis, but Manda can't return a ball nohow. Can you play tennis, Libby?"

"No," Libby said flatly.

"Was it a nice wedding?" Amanda asked. Usually Libby told her immediately when things went wrong. Today she was holding back.

"It was okay. I'm fine, Amanda," Libby reassured her.

"Amanda's mother did my nails. Look." Vera splayed ten fingers out under Libby's nose.

"Umm," Libby said.

"What we ought to do," Vera said, "is have a sleepover club where we sleep over at each other's houses regularly. I'll ask my mother if I can be next. Wouldn't that be fun, Libby?"

"My mother wouldn't go for it," Libby said. "She doesn't—we just don't have the room."

"Oh, I don't mind sleeping on the floor. Do you mind, Amanda?"

"I don't think a club is a good idea," Amanda said, to take the pressure off Libby.

"Okay, if that's the way you feel," Vera said, and her mouth reversed like a turned-over cup.

Libby said kindly, "It's a good idea, Vera. It's just that I can't do it. My mother wouldn't let me."

"Why?"

"She doesn't like—she needs me at home to help weekends."

"But you went to Amanda's house, didn't you?"

"Just once," Libby said.

69

To Amanda's relief, they had to stand and pledge allegiance then and be quiet for the rest of homeroom. She didn't want Vera prying into the details of the painful visit when Libby had failed to measure up to Mother's standards. That Mother could like Vera better than Libby was incredible.

The fifth grade had a special assembly to attend that morning. "Two by two," Mr. Whittier said as they lined up to march to the cafeteria which did double duty as an assembly room. Amanda reached for Libby's hand, but Vera had already taken it. To Amanda's embarrassment, she got stuck walking next to a boy. Worse, Libby and Vera got the last two seats in a row, and Amanda had to walk through the next row back and take the seat furthest away. She stared at the platform, trying to pay attention to the music teacher's students who were demonstrating the instruments they'd learned to play, but she prickled with thoughts. Could Libby be angry at *her* for something? Not too likely. Libby's way was to make excuses for people or forgive them rather than get angry with them. Besides, Amanda couldn't think of anything she'd done.

After sitting still for the long presentation, everybody was impatient to get out of the cafeteria. Pearly was standing in the hall as they burst through the door. "Take your time, angels. Pushing won't make lunch come any faster." She blocked their passage to slow them down.

Amanda heard a teacher behind her murmur sarcastically, "Don't know how we'd run this place without Pearly."

"Don't knock it. She makes our job easier," Mr. Whittier said to him.

"You've got a point," the first teacher admitted.

All the windows were open to let the Indian summer day into the classroom. Mr. Whittier said any students who finished their test early could sit outside on the grass below his window as long as they were quiet and stayed close by.

Usually Amanda needed all the time she was given for math tests, but this one was so easy, she finished early. So did Libby. Vera was still working.

"I thought she was good in math," Amanda said.

"She is, but she told me she always goes over tests twice because her father expects her to get perfect marks. He wants her to be a scientist like he wanted to be when he was a kid. She hasn't told him about going into theater. Her brother's not going to be a scientist either."

Purple asters and wands of pinkish loosestrife grew in the field that started ten feet from the side of the school where they were sitting. Amanda took a deep breath, happy to be outside with her friend on this beautiful last day of September. "We could pick bouquets of flowers for our mothers if we had time before the buses leave," Amanda said.

"Amanda, do you like her better than me?" Libby asked abruptly.

Amanda was so startled that she told the truth. "Are you crazy? I don't like her at all."

"You don't?" Libby's face lit up. "I thought you had such a wonderful weekend with her."

71

"Not really. She liked my family, not me."

"Oh, Amanda. I'm so glad. I was scared you and Vera were going to be best friends and leave me out. I'd hate not being your best friend anymore."

"Was your weekend *really* okay?" Amanda asked.

"It was awful," Libby said. "All they talked about was that the bride's sister was pregnant and didn't have a husband. Oh, Amanda, I liked the bride's sister better than anyone there. Do you think I'm a bad person?"

"I think you're the best person I know," Amanda said truthfully.

Libby hugged her and said with relief, "You're such a good friend." Then she added wistfully, "I wish we didn't have to be friends with Vera."

"Do we have to be?" Amanda asked.

"Well, we can't hurt her feelings, can we?"

"I guess not," Amanda said. "I guess we're stuck with her." Then she confided to Libby, "I don't know what I'd do without you and Pink Pig."

"Pink Pig?"

"You know," Amanda reminded her, "my friend Pink Pig, who's with me when I'm home alone and who goes places with me."

Libby looked at her strangely. "I thought that was one of your stories."

"No," Amanda said simply. "Pink Pig is real." Amanda would have gone on to explain how Wizard was threatening the Little World then, but Vera joined them, sliding her back down the glazed brick of the building to sit next to them.

"Well, I know I aced that one. I checked that test over three times. It was easy, wasn't it?"

72

"Yes," Amanda said.

"Did you see Pearly looking in our classroom for you?" Vera asked.

"What do you mean?" Amanda asked.

"Don't you notice how she tracks you around the school?"

"That's not true," Amanda said. It made her uneasy to think of Pearly spying on her.

"How would you know? You can't even tell real from pretend," Vera said scornfully. "Your brother told me you really believe your miniatures are living things. He thinks you've got such a great imagination, but I think you're crazy. You're too old to have imaginary friends. Right, Libby?"

"I don't have imaginary friends," Amanda said.

"But you just said—" Libby began, and then closed her mouth.

"What?" Vera asked Libby. "What did she just say?"

"Nothing," Libby said. "She knows they're not real. She just pretends."

Amanda's heart pulsed wildly. It hurt to know that even Libby didn't understand. "I don't pretend," Amanda said. "Pink Pig is my best friend." Then because Libby looked at her as if she too now thought Amanda was crazy, Amanda jumped up and raced into the school and up the dim back staircase to their classroom. She sat down in her own seat. Mr. Whittier was marking papers. Only two students were still working. One boy was reading a book. Amanda retrieved Pink Pig from the pencil case.

Patiently Amanda held Pink Pig and waited for her to warm to life. The black hand of the big class clock

73

moved slowly past one minute, two, three. Pink Pig remained hard and glassy and Amanda tightened with fear. Had something happened to her friend? Pink Pig had been worried when the coach had stopped beside them for so long. Had she been right about Wizard's anger? Amanda could hardly wait to get home. She wanted to try and enter the Little World and find out what had happened.

Alone in her bedroom, Amanda stood before her miniature shelf with Pink Pig a lifeless rose quartz figure in her hand. There on the shelf, each one in their proper station, were all the pewter figures—Wizard and Dragon and Boy with the Guitar, Wild Horse and the two knights, one with the horned helmet of a Viking and the other in armor with a visored helmet. The painted bone birds were there and the ceramic duck, and the wooden birds with whimsical dots and stripes like no real bird ever had. Peasant Girl with her baskets of flowers was painted wood and Peasant Man and Peasant Woman painted plaster. Beside the yellow silk giraffe stitched with red and decorated with sequins was the colorful plastic coach with its two brown horses. Next came Ballerina. The green ceramic frog with the smug, human grin, which Dale had given her, lay on its side, its head propped on its elbow. Nothing was missing except Pink Pig. Slowly, holding her breath, Amanda placed Pink Pig in her station, then called to her.

Like being yanked through an open doorway, Amanda was suddenly standing beside Peasant Man and Peasant Woman's house. "Pink Pig!" she screamed when she saw her friend. "Oh, how could he do that to you?"

Pink Pig was chained to a stake in the ground with an iron collar around her plump neck.

"Wizard said I am not to leave the Little World again," Pink Pig said. "And then he forged this collar to make sure I can't."

Amanda was so horrified that she could barely look at her friend who stood bravely enduring her punishment. "What can I do?" Amanda asked.

"Nothing," Pink Pig said. "Wizard chained me and he's the only one who can let me go."

"Frog said I have the power," Amanda said. "I'll go ask Wizard to let you go."

"No," Pink Pig said. "He might hurt you too."

Amanda didn't listen. She ran to the road, but just as she started toward the village, she saw the coach with the two brown horses racing toward her. It terrified her, but she made herself call, "Halt! Stop. I must speak to you." The coach and horses whizzed by as if she weren't there.

"He won't stop unless he wants to," Pink Pig said. "It's no use."

Amanda was determined to help her friend. She ran to the garden where Peasant Man was working with his hoe, took his arm and led him to Pink Pig. Then she borrowed his hoe and showed him how the ground could be chopped away around the stake to loosen it. Even though a shovel would have been better, the hoe worked, especially after Peasant Man understood and lent his muscles to the job.

Before long the stake was loose and Pink Pig could move again, although the collar with the chain and the iron stake hampered her.

"That's much better," Pink Pig said as she wriggled happily from head to twiddly tail. "At least I *feel* free. Thank you."

"You're welcome."

"You know, I couldn't believe that you tried to stop that coach," Pink Pig said. "You really are brave."

"Only because I was angry and acted without thinking. Listen, Pink Pig, we'll have to hide you in my world to keep you safe from Wizard now."

"You mean, stay in your world forever?" Pink Pig asked in alarm.

"Maybe."

"But I couldn't. Your world wears me out. I can't live for long without snoozing in the sun and breathing the special air of the Little World."

"Then what will we do?"

"Frog might have an idea, but I'm too tired to go ask him."

"We had better visit him soon," Amanda said. She returned to her own world for dinner, leaving Pink Pig in the Little World pretending that the stake was still stuck fast in the ground to fool Wizard.

"Ten thousand a year plus for tuition," Dale said, "and that's just for starters, Mom. Why bother applying? We can't afford it, unless you've got a secret bank account somewhere."

All through dinner Dale had been harping on money and how much the various schools Mother wanted him to apply to would cost. Mother didn't seem disturbed even though what Dale said made sense to Amanda.

"Don't worry about it," Mother kept repeating

calmly. She sat straight backed eating her salad sound-lessly with barely visible chewing motions. Amanda tried to imitate her, but concentrating on table manners was hard with Dale so agitated.

Besides, Amanda knew that any minute the doorbell might ring. Vera had invited herself over for the eve-ning. After calling Amanda crazy and upsetting her so much that she had run back into the classroom, Vera had followed Amanda out to her bus, and as if nothing had happened, had said, "I'll get my father to drop me off at your house tonight and we can do our homework together. That social studies chapter won't be so boring if we do it together, right?"

Amanda had been too taken aback to say don't come.

Quietly, Amanda began alerting Mother to the visit. "Vera said she—" but before she had Mother's atten-tion, Dale started in again. He must be really upset to be rude enough to ignore her, Amanda thought.

"A Swiss bank account—that's what you've got, Mom, right?" Dale said. "Or did you just inherit money from some long-lost relative?"

"You'll win an athletic scholarship," Mother said. "And if you don't—"

"Bull!" Dale snapped. "Can't you face it? Your son is not a star, not in sports, not anywhere. Nobody's going to pay to get me."

"You're too modest," Mother said. "You're an out-standing young man."

"And you're as much a dreamer as your daughter is."

"I said not to worry." Mother was losing patience. "Just get accepted by a first-rate school, and I'll pay for it even if you don't get a scholarship."

"But how? How can you swing it? Don't you think I see you juggling bills and dealing with that lousy finance company? You think I'm still a child and that I don't understand how you're struggling?"

"That's in the past. Things are easier now," she said.

"How come? What happened?"

"That's not your business."

"Bull! It *is* my business. Why should I waste my time writing applications to schools we can't afford?"

"You're insulting me," Mother said. "I've told you money's no longer a problem." She hesitated. "I've made some investments, ventured a little capital of my own, and I've been successful."

"Really, Mother? That's great," Dale said. "What kind of investments?"

"I'm just not going to discuss it with you," Mother said. "I'm sorry, but money is something I feel very private about." Suddenly she turned passionate. "Oh, Dale," she said, "money doesn't matter. It's just a means of exchange that anyone can acquire with a little effort. What matters is *you*, that you don't let anything stop you from achieving all you can."

Dale looked gloomy. "Are you going to die of disappointment if I turn out to be ordinary?" he asked.

"You could never be ordinary," Mother assured him. She sounded as elated as when Dale's team won. Dale still looked dejected.

Just then the doorbell rang and Mother went to see who was there. "Vera!" she said. "What a nice surprise. Have you come to see Amanda?"

"She said we could do our homework together here." Vera's voice came confidently. "It's all right, isn't it?"

78

"Fine," Mother said.

"That's a beautiful blouse, Mrs. Bickett," Vera said. "It looks like peacock feathers."

"Thank you," Mother said. "The colors are interesting, aren't they?"

Vera didn't seem in any hurry to get to work. She asked Dale what he thought his team's chances were in the home game on Saturday, and when he barely answered her, she went on undiscouraged to tell him she'd overheard some girl at her bus stop saying that he was not just the handsomest boy in school, but the nicest.

"Maybe we should work in my room," Amanda said to get Vera out of Dale's way. Vera went reluctantly. She didn't seem particularly interested in the social studies assignment.

"Your family doesn't yell at each other, do they?" she asked after she and Amanda had written three of the ten thought questions they had to make up for the chapter.

"Not usually," Amanda said.

"You're so lucky," Vera said wistfully. "My family never stops yelling."

Amanda felt sorry for her until Vera impatiently took the social studies book, and without bothering to consult Amanda, dashed off the rest of the questions they needed. "You can make a neat copy for me while I go talk to your mother, okay?"

"Okay," Amanda reluctantly agreed.

"What does Vera want from me?" Amanda asked Pink Pig that night in the Little World.

"She wants to be your friend."

79

"But I don't think she likes me any better than I like her," Amanda said.

"She says you're lucky. Maybe she wishes she had your mother and brother instead of the ones she's got."

"The real world is very strange, isn't it, Pink Pig?" Amanda said.

"Strange and tiresome," Pink Pig said.

"Has Wizard come by to check on you?"

"He's too busy with his changes. The trouble is pretending to be chained is almost as bad as being chained since I still can't move about. Let's take a chance that he won't notice and go for a walk."

"To Frog's?"

"Not that far. Not so far that I can't run back and push the stake in the ground if I hear the coach coming."

"We'll never stop Wizard if we just wait for what's going to happen next, Pink Pig," Amanda said.

"I'm not worried," Pink Pig said. "You'll think of something. A girl as smart and brave as you can achieve anything."

Usually Pink Pig's praise made Amanda feel good, but tonight it sounded like an echo and brought a strange dread, as if it weren't only Pink Pig's world that was in danger, but her own as well. Whatever power she had in Pink Pig's world, Amanda knew she had none in her own.

Six

Amanda awoke in the night. Someone was howling, "Let me in, Let me in," over and over again.

She reached under her pillow for Pink Pig then remembered Pink Pig was back in the Little World snoozing in the sun. Amanda got out of bed and crept to the window, shivering in the chilly darkness. The round white moon hung so low it looked like an enormous street lamp. It shone on the crazy man across the street. He was banging on his front door and crying. Amanda wished his elderly mother would hurry and unlock the door for him. Instead a siren wailed. A police car pulled up and the crazy man ran, vaulting the fence into his own backyard. Amanda got back under her covers and waited to be warm again. She felt so lonely, as if Wizard were reaching into her world too to make everything hard and cold.

It seemed only a few minutes later that her alarm rang.

Time to get ready for school. She immediately went to the miniature shelf to check on her friend. No Pink Pig. Never before had she been missing. Amanda rechecked the shelf, then picked up everything on her dresser top. She shook out all her bed covers. Pink Pig was gone. Amanda was frantic. She wished she hadn't listened to Pink Pig and allowed her to stay in the Little World.

"Amanda, will you use the bathroom first or shall I?" Mother called.

"You go, Mother." Once again Amanda shook out the covers, crawled around the floor, felt inside the pockets of yesterday's clothes. Then she opened her dresser drawer. Pink Pig's corkscrew tail poked up from a knit shell-pink scarf. With a sigh of relief, Amanda plucked her out.

"How did you get in there?" Amanda asked.

"I don't know." Pink Pig seemed dazed.

Perhaps she had been careless last night and let Pink Pig slip into the drawer, Amanda thought. Or was it a warning from Wizard? She dressed for school, and when it was time to go, asked Pink Pig to come with her.

"I'm afraid to leave," Pink Pig said. "What if he comes by and sees I'm gone? And you don't really need me today. Don't worry. I'm safer here." Reluctantly Amanda left her in her station on the miniature shelf.

"There she is," Vera said to Libby when Amanda walked into class. Libby was wearing the purple hand-me-down sneakers from her brother that she hated. She looked troubled.

"Now ask her," Vera urged. "Go ahead and ask her. You're her best friend. She'll tell you."

"Tell what?" Amanda asked.

"No talking while I take attendance," Mr. Whittier said. Even he sounded grouchy this morning.

"Did you bring your pink pig with you?" Libby asked when they were getting ready to go to gym and could talk again.

"No," Amanda said.

"What's it doing without you?" Vera asked.

"Waiting."

"Amanda," Libby said, "you know it's just a little glass pig, don't you?"

"Rose quartz," Amanda said. "Pink Pig is special."

"But not alive, right?" Libby asked.

"Not to you," Amanda said.

"How about to you?" Vera asked.

Amanda was annoyed. What kind of friends were they to question her as if she were as crazy as the man across the street? Defiantly she said, "Pink Pig does come alive for me, and I like doing things together with her."

"There, I told you," Vera said to Libby.

"Amanda, you *can't* really believe that glass thing's alive," Libby urged as they walked downstairs to gym. "You know it's just pretend. You make up the best stories, and Pink Pig is a story. Tell Vera. Tell her."

"Just because you can't see something doesn't mean it's not real," Amanda said.

"Please, stop it, Amanda!" Libby was almost in tears. "Say that you know the pink pig is not alive. You *do* know it, don't you?"

"She's not alive for you or for Vera," Amanda said. "But she is for you," Vera encouraged her.

"Yes," Amanda said coolly.

Libby groaned.

At lunchtime when Amanda brought her tray with her tuna dreamboat to the table where Vera and Libby were eating their paper-bag lunches, they stopped talking and looked at her. That meant they'd been talking about her. Amanda felt as if she were sitting down with strangers. She asked Libby, "Do you want my pickle?" Libby always wanted her pickle. Today she took it guiltily and hung her head and was silent.

Pearly sailed past them holding up a brown paper bag and yelling, "Somebody's missing their lunch. Ham and cheese and a bright red apple." Her voice rose easily above the hubbub. For a few beats everyone stopped talking. "Found it in the hall on the floor by the lockers," Pearly announced.

"Oh, hey! That's *my* lunch," said a boy leaving the lunch counter line. He looked down in chagrin at the tray of food in his hands. Kids laughed and he grinned in embarrassment and said, "You can keep it, Pearly."

"Thanks, angel." She held up the bag. "Anybody want a ham and cheese sandwich?" Two boys raised their hands and Pearly gave them each half. She winked as she handed the apple to the teacher on lunch duty.

"She has false teeth," Vera said.

"Pearly?" Libby asked. "How do you know?"

"You can always tell. They're too perfect."

"So what if she has false teeth? So what?" Amanda said in sudden disgust with Vera.

84

Amanda wasn't ready to go to the girls' bathroom when they were finished. "We'll wait for you," Libby said.

"You don't have to," Amanda said.

"We'd better go, or there'll be a line and we'll be late for class," Vera told Libby.

"What do you care if you're late?" Libby asked her grumpily. "The worst you can get is detention with your father."

"He'd kill me if I ever got detention," Vera said. "He expects me to be an example to everybody because I'm his daughter."

"That's not fair," Libby said.

"Hurry up," Vera urged and headed down the hall.

"Amanda," Libby began, then stopped as if she wasn't sure what to say.

"Go on," Amanda said. "I'm going to finish my pudding."

Libby looked back once, but Amanda didn't meet her eyes. She wished Pink Pig had come with her. Pink Pig would never leave her feeling bad. Amanda finished her pudding. Then she took her tray to the window, put all the dirty dishes in the right bins and went to the girls' bathroom, more out of habit than necessity.

Three eighth graders were in there writing on the mirror with lipstick. "Thinks she can tell *me* how to act," a girl whose eyes were wreathed in makeup said. "Queen of the toilets, that's what she is. Full of—" Amanda slipped into a stall without their noticing. They were gone when she got out. On the mirror in foot-high lipsticked letters was an ugly sentence with Pearly's name. Amanda shuddered with disgust. She got some toilet paper, but there wasn't any soap, and when she tried rubbing the words off, red grease smeared all over the mirror.

She was working at the mess up as high as she could reach when Pearly walked into the bathroom. Amanda could see her in the mirror. "They wrote something," Amanda said.

"I can see," Pearly said. "You're a good girl to try and wipe it off, but I've got a cleaning fluid will do a better job." When she smiled at Amanda, her cheeks plumped up and her eyes sank in. Her teeth did look very white and even. Amanda picked up her notebook and books and started out.

"Sometime," Pearly said, "you ought to stop by my house for a visit. My house is the one by the underpass with the plaster ducks out in front. You know which one I mean?"

Amanda nodded. Before turning into the school grounds, her bus had to pass the little house that looked like a box with an add-on shed and more sheds in the back of it. Railroad tracks ran across the bridge above it. The house looked very shabby compared to the neat development houses that started up the hill beside it. Amanda wondered if Pearly lived there alone. What would it be like to live alone in a house built of odd pieces of lumber and sections of shingled walls? Would the trains passing by in the night wake her up? What did Pearly do when she wasn't taking care of the school?

"Well," Pearly said, "just remember you got an invitation anytime you want to use it."

"Thank you," Amanda said.

She was late to class. Her teacher sent her down to the office.

"Next time you'll get detention," the secretary said and gave her a pass.

"Did you get detention?" Libby asked her with concern.

"Not yet," Amanda said. She slid into her seat thinking that it wasn't so terrible, after all, to get into trouble.

"Vera says she told your mother about how you think Pink Pig is real, but your mother didn't take her seriously. Vera's going to try again," Libby said when Vera went up front to ask the teacher something. "You'd better not tell your mother any stories about Pink Pig or you'll end up getting your head examined."

"Do you think I'm crazy, Libby?"

Libby considered. "Even if you're crazy, I like you a lot," she said.

Amanda was glad to hear that Libby still liked her. It made her feel a little less alone.

As the bus took her past Pearly's house that afternoon, Amanda thought, why shouldn't she visit Pearly some day? She could walk over after school and then take the late bus home. Mother wouldn't like it. And what would Mother do about that? In school you got detention. At home, there would be a hurt look. Hurt looks were painful, but probably Amanda could survive one.

"How come you're home?" Amanda asked Dale, who was reading at the kitchen table.

"Got to bone up for the SATs. If I don't do better than I did last spring, no school's going to take me no matter how many teams I'm on."

"You mean you won't get into college?"

"Not into any place Mother would approve."

"Then what would happen to you, Dale?"

"Then I wouldn't get into a good law school and I wouldn't get famous and Mother would be disappointed in her wonder boy—I don't want to disappoint her, Manda. She's worked really hard to get us where we are."

"Where are we?"

"Well, you know. We've got a nice home and we know how to behave right. She's given us a good enough start so we can go anywhere in life."

"I don't want to go anywhere special. Do you, Dale?"

"Well, I wouldn't *mind* being a big shot someday. Drive a fancy car and fly my own jet, maybe travel around the world and get written up in the paper. Yeah, I'd like that for sure."

"When I grow up," Amanda said, "I'm going to have my own kitten."

"That's all you want?"

"Well," Amanda said. "Maybe a dog too, and a swing in my own backyard, so I can watch the stars, and a tree so I can hear the leaves whisper."

He laughed. "That sounds simple enough."

"Is it?" she asked. "Good. Maybe I'll get it then . . . I'll go so you can study, Dale."

"You don't have to leave. I like talking to you," he said. "You're an interesting kid, I mean besides being my favorite sister. How about pouring us a glass of milk? We can have some cookies and you can help me figure out some of these tough questions."

Her mouth tasted sweet from the chocolate-chip cookies as she leaned against his shoulder and looked at the book he was reading. Two things were being compared to two things, but she didn't understand what they had in common. He didn't really expect her to help him, but it was nice that he wanted her to keep him company. She rested her cheek against his bony shoulder, loving him.

"Amanda," he said quietly. "I'm not bright enough."

"Yes, you are," she said.

"Mother's sharp, and you are too, but I'm so average it hurts. I must take after our father."

"Wasn't he smart?"

"I don't know. He was quiet, I remember, and nice. But Mother says he was a coward who ran away. I don't know," Dale said. "Maybe I ought to run away too."

"But you're not a coward."

"No . . . I'll give it my best shot. That's the least I can do for her. Maybe the sports will count more than I think." He sighed and pressed his finger on the problem in the book to help him concentrate on figuring it out.

When she was sure he'd forgotten her, she crept to her room. Pink Pig was in place in the shelf waiting for her.

"Where's Wizard?" Amanda asked.

"In his castle as far as I know."

"Good, then we'd better go to Frog now."

89

Amanda used her shoelace to tie the stake to Pink Pig's iron collar so that the stake wouldn't drag on the ground, and they set off. No sooner had they passed Peasant Man and Peasant Woman's fields, than they witnessed the awful changes Wizard had made. On either side of the endless road what had once been fields of flowers were deserts, or leafless woods of weird metal sculptures. When they finally arrived at Frog's pond, they both gasped in horror. The water was now glass, a mirror reflecting the blue sky. It was prettier than the black water had been, but so still, too still. It had the lifelessness of the artificial.

Without waiting for their greeting, Frog said, "The fish have gone. No insects fly. With no food, here soon I will die. Friend Pig, good luck, and Girl, good-bye." He closed his big round eyes and seemed to shrivel inside his pasty skin.

"But you said we had the power." Pink Pig's pinpoint eyes glistened anxiously. "Give us a chance to help."

"Too late, can't wait," Frog said.

"If I could find the coach and make it stop, I'd make Wizard understand that he's wrecking his own world and turning it nasty for himself too," Amanda said.

"The one you really need to help you do the deed is Boy with the Guitar, and he's not very far," Frog told her.

"Promise you won't die on us yet?" Pink Pig asked.

"My situation's dire, but I have no desire to expire," Frog said, adding a "garump" that sounded like a laugh.

"Boy with the Guitar sits on the bridge where the

90

stream sings over the rocks below in tune with his melodies," Pink Pig said. "We should find him there. Hurry!"

Her four legs went so fast that Amanda had trouble following her along the road that narrowed into nothingness. Amanda was remembering that when she had to give an oral report in class, fear always made her voice a whisper no one could hear. Would Wizard hear her even if the coach stopped?

They clattered onto the bridge. Sure enough, Boy with the Guitar sat on the railing lost in his music. He looked up when Pink Pig called to him, then shyly bent his head to his guitar strings instead of meeting Amanda's eyes. Quickly Pink Pig explained what they wanted of him.

"Can you stop the coach with your music?" Amanda asked.

The boy played one sure chord, then strummed a few notes. "That means he can do it, but he's afraid of Wizard," Pink Pig said.

"But so are we," Amanda said. "If we let being scared stop us, this world hasn't a chance of being saved."

"She's right," Pink Pig said to Boy with the Guitar. "We can't afford to be afraid."

Boy with the Guitar looked at the stream, then plucked a single note from his instrument.

"He'll do it," Pink Pig said to Amanda.

"Good. Now all we have to do is find the coach again."

Peasant Girl was coming toward them on the road crying bitterly. No need to ask her why. Her baskets were empty. No more flowers grew anywhere. "Have you seen Wizard?" Pink Pig asked her.

Peasant Girl wiped her tears with the knuckles of one hand, and pointed back the way she'd come with the other.

"Good. The coach should circle the village and return over this bridge," Pink Pig said. She looked at Amanda. "I've been thinking. It would be better if you go, and I wait here and try and stop Wizard by myself."

"Why, Pink Pig? I thought you were afraid."

"Oh, I am, but what if Wizard has the power to hurt you? I couldn't bear it if anything happened to you. As for me, Wizard may kill me, but I'll die anyway when Wizard destroys Peasant Man and Peasant Woman's fields. I have nothing to lose by trying to stop him."

"You're my friend and I can't leave you," Amanda said. "Besides, Frog told us we have the power, we two together."

Pink Pig considered. Finally she said, "All right. We'll face him together . . . It's true I'll be braver if you're with me."

No sooner did she finish speaking than the sound of hoofbeats came faintly, then louder and rapidly more loud. Pink Pig shuddered at the drum roll of hooves. Horses galloped into view. Boy with the Guitar stared wide-eyed with his fingers frozen in the air above his guitar. "Play," Amanda whispered to him. "Start playing now, Boy."

He began with a tune that sounded as bold and colorful as flags waving for a parade. A wise choice,

Amanda thought, because it gave them all courage. She could see the red and gold coach behind the rushing horses now. Boy with the Guitar continued to stare in round-eyed concentration into his music. The horses lifted their forelegs high, prancing in time to the music as Boy played a slow march. Amanda raised her arm and shouted, "Halt, stop. Whoa!" Boy with the Guitar played in a whisper, and miraculously, the horses did slow, snorting and tossing their heads. As they came abreast, they stopped. Their flowing manes and tails stilled and all was quiet.

"You," came a thunderous voice from the coach before Amanda could think of what to say. "How dare you interfere with me?"

"Please," Amanda began. "I must talk to you."

"I don't talk to children," Wizard boomed. "Nor to subjects who dare to escape my rule." The crooked finger appeared in the open window of the coach. Zap, and Pink Pig was gone. The horses whinnied, rose on their hind legs as if they had been whipped, then dashed off.

"Pink Pig!" Amanda screamed. "Pink Pig, where are you?"

"What's the matter with you?" Dale asked, sweeping aside the curtain to her bedroom. "What are you screaming about?"

"Pink Pig is gone," Amanda cried. She was bewildered to find herself standing next to her bed.

"Amanda," Dale said in disgust. "Is that something to get hysterical about? You'll find it. Just look." He went back to his studying in the kitchen. Amanda felt icy. Now Wizard had taken her friend. How was Amanda to get Pink Pig back? Without Pink Pig, she couldn't even enter the Little World. She turned to her miniature shelf. Pink Pig's station was empty, of course. Impulsively, Amanda grabbed the red and gold plastic coach with its two brown plastic horses and put it in her dresser drawer. She almost took Wizard next, but something held her back, a menace that made her shiver even though the room was warm.

"You give me back my friend," Amanda said, "and I'll return your coach to you."

She listened a long while, but heard only the creak of silence.

Seven

Amanda went to bed. She was tired, and all her searching hadn't turned up a rose quartz pig the size of a lima bean. In the morning, she would look again. Even if Wizard could change every bit of the Little World, it didn't seem likely that he could make a solid object that belonged to the real world disappear. Pink Pig might not be alive, but her rose quartz body had to be someplace. Nonetheless, Amanda couldn't find it in the morning. Wearily she got ready for school. It was as good a place as any to think about how to get Pink Pig back from Wizard.

"Amanda, you're not paying attention," the gym teacher snapped. "Libby, see that she gets that floor routine right, will you?"

"What's wrong with you?" Libby asked on their way out of the locker room. "You were daydreaming the whole period."

"Pink Pig is gone."

"Oh, Amanda! I thought it was something really bad."

"It is," Amanda said.

Libby grimaced. "You'll find her again. You probably dropped her in your rug or something like that."

As soon as she got home, Amanda shook the shag rug over her bed. Nothing came out but grains of dirt that the vacuum had missed. Patiently she felt over every inch of yarn. Then she checked behind the curtains and dresser again. Wizard must have hidden Pink Pig somewhere beyond imagining.

Anxiously Amanda fingered the creatures on her miniature shelf one after the other. She picked up Wild Horse and caressed his smooth metal sides. She breathed on him, begging him to speak to her, but in the moist palm of her hand he remained just a pewter figure with one lifted hoof poised as if he were running. Then she tried to coax Boy with a Guitar into life without success. Without Pink Pig nothing was alive. The miniature shelf had lost its magic.

On that long-ago birthday when Pink Pig had come in the mail, Amanda had been sick, and Dale had presented her with a birthday cake in bed so that she could blow out her five green candles. He'd baked the square chocolate cake and decorated it with green and purple roses.

"Brown and green and purple? Dale, what kind of color combination is that?" Mother had laughed.

"Well, so the colors didn't come out right, but it's a nice cake anyway. Right, Mouse?"

It was the first he had ever baked, and she had told him loyally that it was perfect. Then Amanda had

96

opened her presents—stuffed animals, a doll, a battery-operated dog without any batteries from Dale, who'd gotten angry when Mother asked him where the batteries were.

"Why don't you give her the present the mailman brought?" he'd said.

Mother had hesitated, then left the bedroom and returned with a parcel.

"It's from your fairy godmother," Dale had said.

Of course, Amanda had believed him, and she'd opened the small package breathlessly. There was Pink Pig glowing in all her rose quartz beauty right in the center of a wad of absorbent cotton.

When Mother came to kiss her good night, she'd been annoyed to find Pink Pig on Amanda's pillow. "Really, Amanda! Wouldn't one of your stuffed animals or your new doll be more comfortable to sleep with? Besides, you'll lose the miniature if you don't put it someplace like—how about the dresser?" After Mother had left the room, Amanda retrieved the miniature from the dresser top and it was then that Pink Pig had first come to life. Through thousands of lonely minutes, Pink Pig had kept her company. When nobody else understood, Pink Pig did.

"Wizard," Amanda begged the forbidding little pewter figure. "Please, please, please give her back."

"Manda, I think I'm coming down with something," Dale said from the opening in her curtain. "I have the worst headache and aspirin's not helping."

"I'll make you some tea." Mother always suggested tea for sicknesses.

He sat down on her bed and put his head in his hand. "No, thanks. I'm going to lie down. Tell Mother not to wake me up for dinner, okay?" He looked at the miniatures spread out on her dresser. "What are you doing with them now? Your Pink Pig turn up yet?"

"Wizard has her," Amanda said.

"You mean you lost her someplace."

"No, Wizard did something to her."

"Wizard? Amanda," Dale said carefully, "are you making up stories about that little pewter character Mother bought you in the card shop? Come off it, huh? You're too old to be making believe those figures come to life."

"They do."

"That kid you brought here, what was her name? Vera. She said you were acting creepy. She said—you *can't* believe they come alive. You're my sister. You want to end up crazy like the guy across the street?"

"I'm not crazy," Amanda said.

"Well, keep telling people this stuff and they'll think you are."

"I don't care what people think. Wizard got mad at Pink Pig for escaping and I don't know what he did with her."

"Manda, you *do* know the difference between fantasy and reality. You don't really believe—Yes, you do. Oh, boy! Come here, kid."

He held her arms and looked right into her eyes. "The pink pig is a piece of quartz. It can't be alive except in your imagination. Do you believe me?"

Wordlessly she pulled away from him. He groaned and stumbled off to his bedroom holding his head in his hands. She was sorry to have made his headache worse, but she didn't know what to do about it.

Mother came home loaded with packages. "Tonight we're having a gourmet feast," she said happily. "Smorgasbord from the deli."

Amanda wondered what was making Mother act so cheerful lately. "Dale doesn't feel well," Amanda said.

Mother went to his room. Amanda could hear them talking. She laid out on platters the various salads and fish Mother had bought. It made an appetizing-looking display on the table.

"Dale's not hungry," Mother said when she came back to the kitchen. "We might as well eat without him."

She put a sampling of the feast on Amanda's plate. "Taste everything and tell me what you like best."

Amanda picked at her food, obediently trying everything.

"The shrimp salad's delicious," Mother said, "and the smoked sturgeon. It should keep until tomorrow and then Dale may feel more like having some." She put her fork down. "Listen, darling, your brother is very worried about you. He thinks you're—confused. I'm sorry you've lost your favorite miniature. If you like, I'll look for another one like it for you."

"No, thank you," Amanda said.

"Well, will you try to put it out of your mind then? Everyone loses things that are precious to them. Learning to cope with loss is part of growing up, Amanda."

"Wizard has her."

"What?" Mother asked sharply.

"Just because *you* don't believe something doesn't

99

mean it isn't real," Amanda said. "Just because Pink Pig only comes alive for me doesn't make her not alive."

Mother took a deep breath. "What now?" she asked herself. "Oh God, what now?" She clicked her long nails in a rapid rhythm against the top of the table. "Amanda," she said, "Dale thinks I should send you to a psychologist to find out if you're normal." She waited for Amanda to say something. Amanda didn't. "Doesn't that bother you? Do you want to be sent to a doctor?"

"I'm not sick," Amanda said.

Mother sighed and murmured. "I could consult that school psychologist I met at the Business and Professional Women's Club meeting. Olivia Norris was her name. She seemed pleasant enough. And discreet. I'm sure she'd be discreet if I explained—" She focused hard on Amanda and demanded suddenly, "Is Pink Pig real the way you and Dale and I are real?"

"Yes," Amanda said. "But Wizard made her disappear."

Tears filled Mother's vivid blue eyes. "Oh, my God!" she said. "All right. I'll call the woman tomorrow." Amanda felt bad. Mother shouldn't be worrying about her. Dale was the sick one.

Later that evening, Dale walked into her room. She was sitting in the dark, staring out at the street. "Manda, I want to tell you something." He lit her lamp. His face looked too pale with gray smudges under his eyes.

"Are you feeling better?" she asked.

"Listen to me," he said. "Pearly's your fairy god-mother. I mean, you don't have a fairy godmother. I just

100

told you that story because—well, you were a little kid and I thought it was cute that you believed me. See, every year Pearly sends you a miniature for your birthday. She knows Mother doesn't want her to have anything to do with us. So she doesn't put her name or address, but those packages come from her."

"Why doesn't Mother want her to have anything to do with us?"

"Because, well, you know. You've seen her in school. Pearly's not very educated. She dropped out of school in tenth grade and she's loud and she doesn't know how to act right."

"Pearly's nice," Amanda said. "I should thank her."

"Well, she's your grandmother. You know, she came when Dad walked out on us. She offered to help, but Mother got mad. Mother let her have it about what a bum Dad was, and Pearly turned around and said Mother demanded too much of Dad. She called Mother a name. That's when Mother forbid her to ever come near you or me again."

Amanda nodded. "Okay," she said.

"Okay what?"

"I'll thank her for the presents. Maybe she'll know how to get Pink Pig back."

Dale said a bad word and left the room. Amanda turned out the light and slipped into bed. Before she fell asleep, she was comforted by an image of Pearly's warm brown eyes, larger than Pink Pig's black ones but just as kindly.

Vera invited Libby and Amanda to come to her house Saturday afternoon to bake cookies. Libby couldn't go, and Amanda didn't want to go, but Mother said she should.

"You need to spend more time with nice normal kids like Vera. Just go have fun and be quiet about your imaginary world."

Mother had taken time off from work and had gone to see Miss Norris about Amanda. "She says considering how well adjusted Amanda appears to be in school, it's doubtful she's lost touch with reality to a serious degree, but she promised to do an evaluation," Mother told Dale. They both looked at Amanda. Amanda looked away. She had more pressing worries.

In school that day she'd told Pearly about losing Pink Pig. Pearly had looked sympathetic, but just like Mother, she'd said, "I'll see if I can buy you another, angel. I got it from a shop in Florida when I was down there with my sister when she had her attack—God rest her soul. Maybe if I could remember the name of the shop—"

"No," Amanda said. "No, thank you. You don't understand, Pearly. It isn't—I don't want any other pig. I want the one I had."

"But you said it's lost, honey."

Amanda had looked at Pearly silently and walked away.

On Saturday, Mother drove Amanda through the city, then past the park and the small shopping area before the entrance to the interstate highway. There Mother got lost trying to find Vera's development, which was called Birch Estates.

"All these streets look alike," Mother complained after she had stopped to ask for directions and backed up and turned around to cross the main road again. "Aren't you glad we don't live in one of these monotonous-looking developments, Amanda?"

"I don't know," Amanda said. The houses looked nice to her. Most were big and neat with garages built into them and backyards with swingsets and bushes and trees.

"Our home may be small, but at least it's authentic. Beautiful old things increase in value. I suspect I could get twice what I paid for our house if I ever wanted to sell it. Not that I have to now. I've finally had a change of fortune so Dale won't even need a scholarship, and if Miss Norris advises that you need treatment, I can afford to send you. It's nice to have money."

"I'm not sick," Amanda said patiently. She was used to Mother not understanding her; it had always been that way.

Mother glanced at her and then back at the road. "I never know whether you're listening or not, Amanda. Sometimes you make me feel as if I'm talking to myself."

"I'm listening."

"You've always lived too much inside your own head. Dale blames himself. He confessed to me that often when he was supposed to be with you, he's left you alone and gone his own way. Well, he shouldn't have done that, but that can't be the cause. Plenty of children with working parents spend hours alone . . . It could be your imagination is just too vivid. And certainly you're too quiet. You never tell me what you're thinking. Like now. What *are* you thinking, Amanda?"

"I don't want to go to Vera's house without Libby."

Mother made a "tsut" of annoyance. "Well, you're

103

going now that we've come this far," she said. She stopped trying to communicate with Amanda and drove, checking directions against the notes she'd scrawled for herself, until they finally arrived at a gray house with black aluminum shutters and a huge double garage like a gaping mouth. "This is it. Now play whatever she wants to play, and smile for heaven's sake. It might be more fun than you think. And I'll pick you up at four-thirty. Okay?" Mother smiled encouragement as Amanda obediently got out of the car.

As soon as Vera came running out of the house toward them, Mother waved and drove off. Vera looked disappointed. Then she turned to Amanda and said, "We can't bake cookies. We have to stay outside."

It was chilly out. Vera was wearing a ski jacket, but Amanda had only a sweater over a cotton shirt. "Why do we have to stay outside?" Amanda asked.

"Mother's having a fit. She's calling up all Dad's relatives and yelling at them."

"What'd he do?"

"It's what he doesn't do. He doesn't spend time with her or take her anywhere with him. She says he hates her."

Amanda was shivering by the time they'd walked through the neighborhood, and Vera had shown her where all the cute-looking boys lived and pointed out the home of the girl who had a crush on Dale and the one where a high-school girl who wasn't married had had twins. "Isn't that awful?" Vera said.

Amanda supposed it would be hard to take care of babies if you weren't married. For the first time she thought that it must have been hard for Mother after her husband left them.

"I'm awfully cold, Vera," Amanda said.

"Here," Vera said. "Wear my jacket."

"But then you'll be cold."

"We'll take turns with it. I know you want to go back to my house, Amanda, but we can't. See, my mother goes crazy when he goes off with his friends, but he keeps doing it even though he always promises he won't."

"I'm sorry," Amanda said.

"I didn't want you to hear her screaming, but I let the cat out of the bag anyway, didn't I? You won't tell on me, will you?"

"I don't tell people's secrets."

Vera looked embarrassed. "I'm sorry I got your mother and brother on your case. Libby's right. You're a little different, but nice."

"Thank you," Amanda said.

"I wish we could be friends," Vera said. "I know you don't like me much. Nobody does. I don't know why. I'd be a good friend if anybody would let me."

Feeling sorry for Vera, Amanda stretched the truth a little and said, "I like you, Vera. We are friends."

Vera hugged her impulsively. "I don't care if you're crazy. I don't. I love you, Amanda. You and Libby are the nicest kids I've ever met. Come on. Let's run back. That way you'll feel warmer." She zipped Amanda into her coat as if Amanda were a baby or a doll, and they began a ragged run back to the gray house. Vera stood at the door listening.

"I think it's all right now. I can't hear anything. Our family's so loud that Dad always turns the television on full blast when they start a fight to keep the neighbors from hearing."

They walked very quietly through the living room and upstairs. Vera's bedroom was twice as big as Amanda's and the walls were covered with posters. Stuffed animals, large and small, stood on the floor and lay in the chair and on the bed. "Want to make up?" Vera asked.

"Make up?"

"You know, see how you look with eye shadow and lipstick and stuff. I have piles of makeup. Come on, it's fun."

With red spots on her cheeks and a slash of orange on her lips and half moons of green above her eyes, Amanda thought she looked like something from a horror show, but Vera was enthusiastic. "You have to get the hang of it," Vera said. The makeup she put on herself did look more normal. It made her look old though, sixteen at least. Vera seemed pleased when Amanda told her that.

When Mother tooted her horn for Amanda at four-thirty, Vera confessed, "I hated moving here, but now I'm glad. I didn't really have any nice friends where I lived before." She hugged Amanda. "I hope you find Pink Pig again," she said.

Amanda went to the kitchen and politely thanked Vera's mother for the crackers and juice they'd had earlier. Vera's mother gave her an absent smile and said she must come again soon. Amanda ran out to the car feeling guilty because she was relieved to be going. Poor Vera, she thought. Libby and she would have to stick by her even if she wasn't too likeable.

"Did you have a nice time?" Mother asked.

"Sort of," Amanda said.

"Good," Mother said. "I went shopping. I bought you a new winter coat. Your old one probably still fits you, but wait until you see this one. It's got a fur collar. You should love that."

"Yes, thank you," Amanda said. She hoped Mother wouldn't make her get rid of her comfortable old coat. She liked old clothes. Rather than making her look different, they helped her look like herself. But it was good of Mother to buy her things, and the new coat *was* beautiful. Amanda smiled for Mother when she tried it on.

"What a sad smile!" Mother said. "Are you getting sick again, Amanda?"

"Maybe," Amanda said. She didn't know if it was an outside or an inside sickness, but something was making her feel as if she had an empty hole in her middle.

Eight

Mr. Whittier looked annoyed at the message the eighth grader handed him. "Guidance wants you pronto, Amanda," he said. "Ask them to introduce you to division with decimals since that's what they're making you miss this period."

She looked at him wide-eyed. Did he really mean her to ask such a question?

"Oh, go on," he said. "I'll catch you up after school today. I've got to stay for a meeting anyway."

Embarrassed at being singled out, she ducked her head and hurried off to Guidance. There she discovered that she'd been sent for by the psychologist who only visited their school twice a week. Mother had called, Amanda remembered, but that had been more than a week ago. The purse-mouthed secretary sent Amanda into a small office where she was smiled at by a bony, serious-looking young woman with sparse brown hair who asked her to sit down. Amanda gave an uncertain smile back and sat down.

"Don't worry," the psychologist said. "All I'm going to do is ask you questions that I guarantee you'll know the answers to. My name is Miss Norris. And you're Amanda Bickett, right?"

"Yes," Amanda admitted, and waited for the questions to get harder.

"Now these tests are not going to have any effect on your schoolwork, Amanda, and nobody needs to know about them except you, your mother and me. Okay?"

Amanda nodded. She wondered why they had to be secret. Then she realized that if she were crazy, Mother wouldn't want anybody to know. Miss Norris continued talking, explaining things as if she were already asking questions. "No right or wrong answers. . . . ?"

Amanda got more and more tense. These might be trick questions like riddles or jokes which she always got wrong. And despite Miss Norris's "don't be nervous" tone of voice, Amanda was sure her answers were going to affect her, especially if they made Miss Norris decide she was crazy.

For the first test, Miss Norris showed her pictures of people—a mother and child, a little boy in a doorway. Amanda was supposed to make up stories about them. The pictures looked sad but she tried to make the stories happy. "The little boy would like a pet," Amanda said. "He's wondering what kind of pet to ask his father for when he gets home from work. His father's coming home soon and the little boy will be happy to see him." She looked at Miss Norris to gauge her reaction to that, but Miss Norris wasn't giving away any clues to what she thought.

"That was an interesting story," Miss Norris said, "but why didn't the boy ask his *mother* if he could have a pet?"

"His mother's gone. He lives with just his father."

"And who's taking care of him while his father's at work?"

"Well, nobody. He takes care of himself."

"And how does he feel about that?"

"He doesn't mind," Amanda said.

"He doesn't? Oh, well, why does he want a pet?"

"To love," Amanda said, "and to be with."

After they'd gone through a pile of pictures and a bigger pile of questions, Amanda said, "Gym comes after math, and I'd better not miss it."

"Oh, you have lots of time before the next period," Miss Norris said. "How about drawing some pictures for me now?"

Miss Norris wanted Amanda to draw a house, and then a tree, and then a person. Amanda drew Vera's house with a huge garage in front and a big bay living-room window. The tree she drew was the one outside her own bedroom window. She made it heavy with leaves although the real ones had already turned golden and fallen. For the person, Amanda drew herself with long stringy hair and sneakers and pants. The figure could have been a boy's except for the long hair, and since Amanda didn't want to make any mistakes, she added fancy sleeves on the shirt to show it was a girl.

"Can I go now?" she asked when she'd finished.

"Why are you in such a rush? Aren't you having fun

110

here with me?" Miss Norris coaxed. Amanda shrugged, then offered a small smile in apology.

"There's one more test I'd like to give you before you go to gym, but if you'd rather come back—" Miss Norris said.

"No, thank you," Amanda said. "I'll stay." Better get the whole thing over with now and not have to come back.

She was certain that she'd spent hours with Miss Norris and was amazed to find herself on time for gym when Miss Norris finally released her.

"What did Guidance want you for?" Vera asked while they were getting into their gym shorts and sneakers.

"I had to take some tests."

"Did you pass them?"

"I don't know. Miss Norris says there're no right answers."

"Oh, oh," Vera said. "Norris is the school psychologist. I bet your mother asked her to test you to find out if you're crazy."

"Amanda's not crazy," Libby said.

"Well, anyone who thinks a glass pig is real isn't normal," Vera said.

"What did you tell her, Amanda?" Libby asked anxiously. "Did you talk about Pink Pig?"

"She didn't ask me," Amanda said.

"Well, what are you going to say if she does?" Libby wanted to know.

"You better lie if she asks you about that glass pig," Vera said. "If you don't, you'll get in big trouble."

"You're the one who got her in trouble," Libby said. "You started the whole thing."

"I did not. I just said it to her brother and mother. *I* didn't tell the psychologist on her."

"What are you going to do?" Libby asked Amanda, looking worried. "Do you think you can lie?"

"I don't know," Amanda said.

"It's easy," Vera encouraged her. "All you have to say is you were just kidding around and you know it's glass."

"Pink Pig is gone anyway," Amanda said. She felt sad and apart where her friends' concern couldn't reach her.

After lunch she saw Pearly chatting with some eighth graders in the hall. "I remember you when you was nothing but a pint-size mischief, and look at how good you turned out," Pearly said.

"That's because you kept telling me what an angel I was," answered the boy, whose face still twinkled with mischief. "You brainwashed me, Pearly."

"All you children are angels," Pearly said. "Except when you're doing something you oughtn't. Well, good luck in your new school, and don't forget to let us know how you like it."

The boy shook her hand and waved as he walked off with his friends.

Amanda smiled at Pearly and said, "Hi," shyly.

"What's wrong?" Pearly said. "You look like you lost your best friend."

"Well, I did," Amanda said. She would have liked to talk it over with Pearly, but the bell rang and she had to hurry off to class.

At the end of the day, she was halfway to the bus before she remembered she had to stay with Mr. Whittier. Suddenly she felt angry, angry at her mother and

Dale. Vera didn't know her very well, but a mother and brother should know she wasn't crazy.

Mr. Whittier got right down to business. In no time at all, he had her doing division with decimals. "It's easy," Amanda said with surprise.

"Of course it is," Mr. Whittier said. "Especially when you've got your private teacher to give you instant feedback." He smiled at her and added, "You're better at math than you think, Amanda."

She trailed out of his room feeling fine. She had almost an hour to wait for the late bus. Dale would wonder what had happened to her if he got home and didn't find her there. On the other hand, he probably wouldn't be home on time either. Impulsively, Amanda walked out of the school and started down the road toward the underpass. So what if Mother was angry that she'd visited Pearly. She shouldn't have gotten Amanda in trouble with Miss Norris.

Pearly's house looked like a clubhouse children might have built, with patched-on additions that didn't fit in shape or color. Amanda had a hard time finding the front door. She walked past the plaster duck and ducklings and stopped in confusion. Then a kitten came around the side of the house and stepped gravely, tail up, toward her. It stopped just out of her reach, sat down and licked its front paw. Amanda crouched and cooed at the kitten. It studied her and meowed. Cautiously Amanda moved closer and touched the deliciously soft fur. The kitten pushed its head up against Amanda's fingers. Then the sharp little claws were digging for a hold against Amanda's knee and the kitten climbed onto her shoulder. Amanda laughed with pleasure.

"Bold one, isn't he?" Pearly said, appearing suddenly in the yard. "His sister's shy as can be and hides under the table if you so much as look at her, but he likes people."

"What's his name?" Amanda asked.

"Haven't named him," Pearly said. "His mother's name was Sunny because she was as yellow as a sunny afternoon. Car hit her. Why don't you come inside and I'll make you a cup of hot chocolate or something, Amanda?"

Amanda got up carefully with the kitten wound in her hair and followed Pearly around the corner of the green-shingled main part of the house. The front door was on the side next to a woodpile. A cage with plump white rabbits was next to the woodpile.

"Oh," Amanda said. "What cute rabbits!"

"Flopsy and Mopsy," Pearly said. "Them two are something. I let them hop around the house with the kittens and you'd think they was all the best of friends. They got no fear of those cats yet, none at all."

"Can I take one in?"

"Sure you can. Mopsy is the one with the brown patch over his eye, and Flopsy is the fatty over there."

Pearly brought in Mopsy at Amanda's direction. The kitchen was crowded with objects and smelled of wood smoke—jars of flower cuttings and cans planted with green growing things, shelves of canned fruits and vegetables and an assortment of ceramic jars, a teapot, a colander filled with bananas. Pots hung on the wall.

The only appliance Amanda recognized was the refrigerator.

"Bet you never seen a wood stove like this one," Pearly said. She picked up a small log and pried open a lid on an enormous black iron hulk which had a pipe as big as Amanda's body leading up into the ceiling. A fire was going inside the stove. "This old thing heats my house and cooks my dinner," Pearly said. "Makes hot water too when my heater runs out. Hot chocolate all right? Course you could have tea or soup or something cold to drink if you'd rather."

"Hot chocolate sounds good," Amanda said. Everything looked clean enough to satisfy Mother, despite the messy appearance of the room. Amanda sat on the floor and the kitten jumped off her and strutted up to the rabbit, who hopped over to a bowl of food. The kitten put his paw on the rabbit's cotton-ball tail which made Amanda laugh out loud.

"So what were you looking sad about today?" Pearly asked as she poured milk into a pot.

"You don't think I'm crazy, do you, Pearly?" Amanda asked.

"Course you're not," Pearly said. "Inside a person's own head, all kinds of things is real. Sometimes in the winter I hear voices talking to me. Of course, I know it's just the wind, but I could let myself think they was real if I wasn't careful."

"Would you lie if a psychologist asked you questions?"

"Lie about what?"

"About what you believe that other people think is crazy."

115

"You mean like you thinking that little quartz pig was real? I don't know. Lying is bad for your own self-respect. On the other hand, why get everybody all worked up over something that's lost anyhow?"

"I didn't lose her. Wizard captured her."

Pearly sighed. "You sure have a vivid imagination."

"But that doesn't make me crazy."

"I don't know, angel. Most of us is a little off one way or another." Pearly set the hot chocolate in a mug in front of Amanda and asked if she wanted a squirt of canned whipped cream on top. Amanda said that would be nice. It was comforting to think her craziness was common. She cuddled the rabbit, who was the softest, silkiest creature Amanda had ever touched, but after a minute the rabbit squirmed free. It had strong muscles underneath the softness. Amanda sipped her hot chocolate. It tasted wonderful.

"You know," Pearly said, "when Dale come to middle school, I tried to make friends with him, but he didn't want no part of me. I didn't know if you'd be any different. I always wanted to get to know my grandkids. I guess I've made lots of talks in my head with you. Maybe that's crazy too, imagining you sitting here—just like you really are now—and us talking." Pearly shook her head, smiling her apple-cheeked smile. Then she said, "I kept all Dale's school pictures. The secretary let me order copies special. Want to see them?"

Amanda followed her up two steps into a room which had a couch with sprung seats. Pieces of lace and a knitted throw cover hid its basic fabric. Stacks of magazines and papers covered a table, and in the corner was a barrel-like stove with a tall china cat perched on top of

116

it. The kitten had hold of Amanda's shoelace. She giggled when it pulled out the bow. "Here," Pearly said as she dug an album out from the pile on the table. "My family photo album. See, I don't have any pictures of you yet because you just got to the middle school. But here's Dale's from all four years."

"Yes," Amanda said. "We have those at home."

"He's a handsome boy," Pearly said proudly, "good athlete too, like his father was."

"Do I look like my father, Pearly?" Amanda held her breath. She had never dared ask Mother.

"You look like yourself. You're a pretty girl," Pearly said. Her eyes were bright on Amanda. "Roland was a good boy, a sweet boy, but he wasn't handsome. Plain faced, like me. Here, I'll show you a picture of him. I guess your ma don't keep none."

"No," Amanda said. "She doesn't."

"Well, she's mad at him because he left her, and maybe he should have stuck it out. Still, I think it's mostly her pride he hurt by leaving. She sure didn't think much of him when she had him."

The picture was of a lanky young man standing under a tree. All that could be seen of his face was his grin. "That was took before he went in the army. He put on weight in the army and looked real good in his uniform."

"Where did he go after the army?" Amanda asked.

"Alaska, first. Then he worked on oil rigs some. Got killed working on an oil rig. It tipped over in a storm a few years back."

"Mother didn't say how he died," Amanda said.

"She didn't? Now isn't that something! She knew

117

because of the insurance. It come to her, of course. Don't Dale know either?"

"I don't think so," Amanda said. "He never said anything, but he doesn't always tell me things."

"Don't they talk to you, Dale and your ma?"

"Well—not about everything. Not all the things I'd like to know."

"Probably they forget you're not a baby anymore. That happens when one child's so much younger."

"Yes," Amanda said. She felt grown-up sitting next to Pearly, having a conversation about important things. She felt comfortable.

"Well," Pearly said when they had closed the photo album. "There's a lot I could still show you, but you better be getting home. Your brother know where you are?"

"No," Amanda said. "I'll get the late bus and probably get home before him."

"Oh, angel, you already missed the late bus, but don't worry. I'll drive you," Pearly said. Amanda looked at the clock in the kitchen and couldn't believe how late it was. The time that had dragged in the psychologist's office had flown by in Pearly's house.

Amanda couldn't take the lively kitten on her lap in Pearly's big old car, but the fat white rabbit seemed content to sit and be fed a carrot while Pearly drove and Amanda petted. "I love animals," Amanda said.

"What kind of pets do you have at home?" Pearly asked.

"Dale gave me a turtle once, but it died," Amanda said.

"Your mother don't like pets?"

"She says our house is too small. I hope I can come to visit you again sometime, Pearly. I had a really fun time."

"I did too," Pearly said. "You going to tell your mother where you were?"

"Yes."

Pearly sighed and smiled. "You're something, you are. You're quite a girl, Amanda."

"I don't like to lie, but I think I'll try to with Miss Norris, at least if she asks about Pink Pig."

"You really think that miniature I sent you is alive?"

"Well, she was, but she's been gone so long now." Amanda felt strange as she spoke, as if all of a sudden she wasn't sure of what she was saying. Here was Pearly, who was her grandmother, whom Dale had once called her fairy godmother, and Pearly clearly did not believe that a pink quartz pig could be transformed into a living being. Suppose it *had* been all in Amanda's imagination? Suppose Pink Pig never had come alive?

"The thing is," Pearly said, "people who think pretend things are real, they're thought to be a little crazy. But being crazy's not so bad, not so bad as being mean, for instance. And what's in your head can get straightened out. That's what them psychologists are for."

Pearly let Amanda out in front of her house. "See you in school tomorrow," Pearly said. "Good night, angel, and don't worry. You're going to be just fine, a good girl like you. Of course you are."

Pearly's fond look and the softness of the rabbit stayed with Amanda as she walked into the house. Along with Pearly's promise, they made Amanda feel "just fine."

119

Nine

Even before Amanda stepped inside the house, she heard Mother's voice. ". . . Not your business to question me about money." The voice sounded fierce but edged with tears. "A netsuke like this will increase in value. It's an investment, and if I want to treat myself to something beautiful, why shouldn't I?"

"I just don't understand," Dale said, "how all of a sudden you've got cash enough to buy out the clothing stores for us, and now you can even afford to start a collection of netsukes. That's ivory, isn't it, like the one you showed me that cost hundreds of dollars in the antique store? Did somebody die and leave us a pile of money?"

Amanda stood in the living room watching them face each other from either end of the couch, like twin male and female bookends. The object they were discussing was a soapy oriental figure the size of a baby's fist on the cocktail table. It wasn't even pretty. Amanda waited for them to notice her, ready to explain why she'd gone to visit Pearly. "I wanted to see what my grandmother was like," she would tell them.

Finally Dale turned and said, "There you are, Manda. The late bus was really late, huh? Whittier give you a hard time?"

"No," Amanda said, confused that he knew about Mr. Whittier.

"How did your session with Miss Norris go?" Mother asked, absently as if her mind was still focused on her argument with Dale.

"She asked me a lot of questions," Amanda said.

"Did she say anything?"

"That the answers wouldn't count."

Mother sighed. "Why don't you set the table, Manda," she said. "I brought home some barbecued chicken, and you can open a can of peas too."

"Mr. Whittier didn't take very long to teach me division with decimals," Amanda began; she would have continued but Mother interrupted her.

"We know, Manda. Dale called your friend Libby when you didn't get home, and Libby explained that you had to stay after."

"Yes," Amanda said. "But after—"

"Manda," Mother said brightly. "Wouldn't it be fun to go shopping for a suit for your big brother tonight? He doesn't think it's important to look impressive for those college interviews, but we know better, don't we?"

"Look, I'd be happy to own a good suit," Dale said. "That's not the point. The point is I can't figure out why

121

money was a problem this summer and it isn't now. How much did you make on those investments anyway?"

"You don't have to know everything," Mother screamed so suddenly that Amanda jumped and even Dale looked startled. "I'm the sole provider in this family, and I'm providing very well. I deserve appreciation from you, not criticism and suspicion."

"Mom, I'm not criticizing you," Dale said. "I'm just worried that—"

"*Don't* worry. Don't you worry about anything," Mother said. Amanda had never seen her look so strange and was glad to escape to the kitchen where she could bury their voices under a clatter of silverware and dishes.

They ate dinner in a tight silence. Mother wasn't talking. Dale mentioned the arrangements he'd made to get to the game Saturday, but nothing else was said. Not the time to bring up Pearly, Amanda decided. Mother was already too upset.

After helping Dale do the dishes, Amanda went to her room. She stared at the empty station on the miniature shelf where Pink Pig should have been. How lonely it was without her, worse than when her after-school baby-sitter had moved away last spring and Amanda had had to get used to coming into the house alone. Even the biggest stack of library books hadn't filled the echoing emptiness of that hour before Dale got home from high school. She used to turn the television on, not to watch its mind-dulling programs, but to hear human voices in the house.

"Pink Pig," Amanda whispered, "what did Wizard do to you?" She knew that her friend would never leave her

122

voluntarily. Wizard had punished Pink Pig somehow. If only the punishment had a limit, if only Pink Pig would return.

Amanda was pulling her dresser away from the wall when Dale poked his head into her room. "What are you up to, Mouse?"

"Looking for Pink Pig."

"Still? You don't give up easy, do you? Come on. Mother wants us to go clothes shopping."

"I want to stay here."

"You can't stay home alone."

"Why not?" she asked. "I do every day."

He winced. Then he shrugged. "She won't like it," he said and left.

He came back as Amanda was crouching to look behind the dresser.

"Mother says you have to come with us, Manda. She's waiting outside in the car."

Amanda couldn't believe her eyes. There lay Pink Pig, upside down on top of the molding behind the dresser.

Sitting in a chair in the men's store, Amanda kept touching the hard rose quartz body and watching it anxiously for signs of life. Mother and Dale were listening to the enthusiastic salesman rattle on about soft weaves and hard weaves, single-breasted vs. double-breasted, and about how Dale needed the width in the shoulders. Amanda's joy at finding Pink Pig had turned to dread that only her friend's lifeless body had been returned.

"Amanda, come see how dashing Dale looks in this gray flannel," Mother called. She sounded happy again.

Amanda joined her at the mirror where Dale was standing.

"The truth is, a handsome fellow like your son makes any suit look good," the salesman said. "And anyone can see where he gets his looks from."

Mother's smile was radiant. Over Dale's protests, she insisted on buying him two expensive ties and shirts to go with the suit. "And shoes," she said. "Tomorrow night, we'll go shopping for a pair of dress shoes."

Lying in her bed in the shadowy room later, Amanda stroked Pink Pig's glassy body with one forefinger over and over and over. She only gave up when sleep caught her and she fell into a half doze. That was the instant Pink Pig chose to appear.

"What happened to you?" Amanda asked. "I thought you were lost forever."

Pink Pig seemed dazed. "I don't know what happened. I think I was trapped somewhere dark. How long have I been gone?"

"Weeks," Amanda said. She was glad to see that the hideous iron collar and chain were gone.

"Come," Pink Pig said urgently. "Let's find out what has happened."

They stood beside Peasant Man and Peasant Woman's cottage. The old couple sat side by side on the bench next to their front door. Amanda had never seen them sitting together, doing nothing. Their lined faces looked sadder than ever. Around them in every direction stretched the whiteness of snow-covered land where there had never been snow before. The vegetable garden, the corn field, sheds and barns, Pink Pig's pen, all were smoothed over, deleted by snow.

"Now look what he's done," Pink Pig said. "It has never snowed in the Little World. It was always summer here."

The road arrowed into the empty distance with dead land on either side. No bird calls. No flutter of wings in the air. No flowers to color the world brightly—only the brilliant blue sky with the sheet of frozen white earth below.

Amanda was angry. "It's time I taught Wizard a lesson," she said. "Let's go back to my world. I'm going to take him off the shelf."

"No, please!" Pink Pig said. "Before you risk it, let's at least ask Frog what he thinks of the idea."

"Suppose we meet Wizard on the way and he decides to get rid of you for good?"

"I'll hear him coming and hide."

Without giving Amanda a chance to wonder where in that bleak landscape a hiding place could be found, Pink Pig set off down the road to Frog's pond. Amanda had no choice but to follow. She didn't hope for much help from Frog, but, nevertheless, when they arrived at the mirror that had used to be Frog's pond, she was shocked to find Frog gone.

"Where could he be?" Amanda asked.

"Without his pond? He could be dead," Pink Pig said grimly, "just the way Peasant Man and Peasant Woman and all the rest of us will die without the vegetable garden and fields to feed us. It's over. Wizard has destroyed the Little World. Unless—"

"Unless what?"

"We haven't tried Wild Horse. Maybe he could help."

"How could he?"

"I don't know. But he's the only one left to ask. I don't want you to touch Wizard. Suppose he has more power than you and gets so angry that he does something terrible to you?" Pink Pig said.

Amanda looked at Pink Pig's loving face, thinking that the worst Wizard could do to her was to steal her friend forever.

"We'll try Wild Horse first, and if that doesn't work, I'll deal with Wizard my way," she said.

"You are different somehow," Pink Pig said wonderingly. "You seem stronger. Have I been gone so long that you've grown up?"

"Not yet," Amanda said. "Now let's go find Wild Horse before Wizard finds you." Pink Pig headed straight across the snowy fields, leaving a pattern of small hoofprints to follow.

They passed through the sculptured woods, dodging the sharp edges of metallic branches. "It seems he's left nothing natural," Amanda said when they stopped to catch their breaths. She thought of Mother, who also preferred the artful to the natural. Amanda didn't. "Are we near Wild Horse yet?"

"Yes, very near, I think."

"Good, then why don't you stay here and let me go on alone?" Amanda said. "This woods would be a good place for you to hide."

Pink Pig's eyes were black points of fear, but she said, "No, I'll take you to Wild Horse, and then run back here if I have to."

"I'm older and you've gotten braver," Amanda said.

They emerged from the woods and faced a snowy hill. Wild Horse stood on the crest, looking magnificent against the blue sky. His shoulders rippled with muscle and his mane fell luxuriantly over his neck while his large dark eyes regarded them proudly.

Amanda started to speak, but Wild Horse interrupted her. "I know why you've come. But I must warn you Wizard has his knights out looking for you two. The knights treat rebels harshly. You are in mortal danger."

"I thought you were Wizard's friend," Pink Pig said suspiciously.

"He's ruined my grassy fields with this crystal white stuff in which nothing grows. He's no friend of mine."

"Will you take me to Wizard?" Amanda asked Wild Horse.

Wild Horse hesitated, then said, "I fear the knights, their sword and lance, and if I help you, I must fear Wizard too."

"Can you live in these snow fields?"

"No," Wild Horse admitted. "Very well." He walked down the hill and knelt on his front legs so that Amanda could climb onto his back.

"But what can you do unarmed against the knights?" Pink Pig asked her.

"You go and hide," Amanda said confidently. "I'll do something." Her anger at Wizard made her feel powerful. Besides, she didn't want Pink Pig to worry.

Reluctantly Pink Pig retreated into the woods. Amanda waited until she couldn't see her friend anymore, then told Wild Horse she was ready to go.

"I hear them," Wild Horse said. "They're marching toward us."

He cantered back up the hill and stopped at the crest. Soon even Amanda could hear the tramp of marching feet. Wild Horse neighed and reared, turning to run away, but no sooner did he set off, than the knights appeared from that direction, pounding toward them in a fearsome clang of armor and heavy booted feet. Wild Horse swerved to go another way, but the same knights appeared there, even closer than before and more awesome with their weapons aimed and ready. Frantically Wild Horse whirled round and round, but wherever he set off, the knights loomed closer. Right behind them came a dense gray fog.

Fear filled Amanda too as the knights approached. One had Viking horns on his helmet and carried a sword. His massive head was covered with coarse blond hair and beard. The second knight wore armor. In one hand he carried a shield and in the other a lance.

"Halt!" Amanda commanded. She extended her arm, palm out. Power surged through her.

Wild Horse stood still, snorting as the knights advanced. "Wizard, I warn you, I will throw you out of the Little World forever if you do not restore it," Amanda said in a ringing voice.

The knights stopped and stood aside. The fog grew. It became misty and stretched and spread until it towered like a tornado against the sky. Inside the swirling mist appeared the powerful, awesome form of Wizard.

Amanda had never felt smaller. Still she stood firm believing that if she wavered now, all was lost. For a long while, the towering gray mass threatened to topple and smother her, but a ghostly horrible weaving began like moiling clouds just before a storm. The evil presence stretched toward Amanda. She didn't move. It came within a hair of reaching her outstretched palm.

She could hear Pink Pig squealing in terror from a distance. Suddenly the cloud disappeared. There stood Wizard, gray face twisting beneath his gray pointed hat and robe.

"You stole my coach," Wizard screamed. "Return it or else."

"You can have it back on two conditions. First, promise never to harm Pink Pig again, and second, change the Little World back to the way it was." It amazed her to find that she wasn't afraid of Wizard. She had power too, and the courage to use it.

Slowly Wizard's crooked finger aimed at Amanda's heart. His eyes burned hatefully. Amanda reached out and grabbed his finger. The world whirled around her in a dizzying frenzy. Round and round. Finally she opened her eyes to find herself in darkness.

She was standing in her own room. She looked toward her window, which was shiny with light from the street lamp reaching through the bare branches of the trees outside. Then she screamed. Pressed against the glass was the flattened face of the crazy man from across the street. She screamed again.

"What's the matter?" Dale swished her curtain wall aside. "Are you all right?"

She pointed. The face was gone. Dale went to the window, raised it and looked outside. "What'd you see? Nothing's outside."

"The crazy man," Amanda gasped. "He was looking in."

"Well, he's not here now. Don't be scared. I'll check the bushes," Dale said. He kissed her forehead and she clung to him.

"What's going on?" Mother asked. "I was sleeping, and—What's the matter with Amanda?"

"Nothing," Dale said. "The guy across the street scared her. He looked in the window or something."

"Oh my God!" Mother said. "Should we call the police, Dale?"

"I don't know. The guy's supposed to be harmless. Besides, we can't be sure. Maybe Amanda was dreaming."

"It's time we sold this house and moved to a safer neighborhood. We're too close to the center city here, and Amanda's getting older."

"Now I really know you've flipped out. I don't need to worry about getting scholarships because you can afford a fortune for my college education. New clothes, doodads, and now you're saying you can go for a house in a better neighborhood too? What did you do, Mother, rob the bank?"

Amanda looked at her mother who froze. After a long minute, Mother said, "I will not tolerate being spoken to like that, Dale."

In the end, Mother called the crazy man's mother and explained that he had frightened Amanda. Afterwards, she reported to Dale and Amanda, "She said we should call the police, and not bother her. She said she has no control over her son." Firmly Mother announced, "This weekend I'll start looking for a house someplace where Amanda can go out alone without my worrying. You'd like a bigger house, wouldn't you, darling?" Mother asked Amanda.

As soon as she was alone in the dark again, Amanda relaxed her fingers. She had been clutching the thimble-sized figure of Wizard. In her hand he was just a pewter figurine, nothing to fear. Quietly she slipped from her bed and opened her window. Then she tossed Wizard out into the bush that crowded the front door steps and she returned to bed. In no time, she was sound asleep.

Miss Norris sent a notice to homeroom giving Amanda an appointment for mid-November, almost a month away.

"I guess you're not very crazy," Libby said, "or she wouldn't wait a whole month to see you again."

"*You* said Amanda wasn't crazy at all," Vera said.

"She isn't. I was just kidding."

They had to work in pairs to research Australia in the library for social studies. "Listen, Vera," Libby said after the teacher refused to let them be a trio. "Amanda and I always work together. You can find someone else for just this project, can't you?"

"That's not fair," Vera said. "I think we should flip a coin for who works together. The two that match make a pair."

"It could all come up heads, or all come up tails," Libby said.

"Then we flip again."

"What do you say, Amanda?" Libby asked.

"It's okay," Amanda said. If the teacher didn't assign her a partner, she could do the research by herself. Kangaroos would be interesting to study.

Heads was odd man out. Libby got it. "Oh, fish bones and potato peels," she said. That was her latest expression when she was upset enough to curse. "Now who will I ask?"

"You could ask Marvin," Vera said. "He's smart and he doesn't have any friends."

"You ask him for me," Libby said. Vera promptly got up and walked across the room to Marvin who was doodling on his notebook. He glanced toward where Libby and Amanda were sitting and nodded.

"Well," Libby said to Amanda. "Wish me luck. I guess I'll get a good grade at least." Vera waved her over encouragingly, and Libby picked up her notebook and moved to Marvin's desk.

"There, that takes care of that," Vera said. She plunked herself back down in her seat and smiled at Amanda. "Let's get the books we need from the library and start work over at your house after school today, okay?"

"Not today," Amanda said. She didn't want Vera visiting this afternoon. First of all, Amanda wanted to be free to find out what had happened in the Little World since she had gotten rid of Wizard. And then, Mother and Dale might still be angry with each other. Amanda didn't want Vera to see them fighting. Even if Vera was a friend, Amanda didn't quite trust her with secrets. Quickly she decided and told Vera, "I'm going to visit my grandmother this afternoon."

"Your grandmother. You mean Pearly? I thought you didn't have anything to do with her."

"I visited her once. I'm going again."

"Pearly! Wow," Vera said and her eyes widened. "Does your mother know?"

"Not yet."

"She won't like it. I bet you she won't let you."

Amanda didn't answer. Vera was right. Mother

132

wasn't going to like it. The thing to consider was whether it was all right not to tell her, at least not until Amanda had had a chance to get to know Pearly better. If Amanda was lucky, Mother wouldn't be ready to listen to her. Then Amanda wouldn't need to tell her anything.

Ten

Amanda said she'd like to visit after school. Pearly looked delighted but she told Amanda to use the school phone to call home first. "I don't have a phone," Pearly explained. "Course I can use my neighbor's. Her and me trade—home-baked pies and vegetables from my garden for the use of her phone—but I don't like to take advantage."

Since Dale wasn't at home, Amanda tried to reach her mother at the bank, but was told she was busy. So Amanda left a message that she'd be late. "Well, now," Pearly said happily. "The kittens will be glad to see you."

The kittens were always glad to see Amanda on the frequent after-school visits she began to make to Pearly's house, so were the rabbits, and so was Pearly. She had a way of making Amanda feel special. "Aren't you smart to know that," she'd say, or, "Don't you look pretty today."

They had mini-conversations whenever their paths crossed in the halls at school, and twice they'd shared a private lunch in the kitchen of the home arts room which the home arts teacher had told Pearly she was welcome to use when classes weren't being held there. Pearly liked to talk about people and puzzle out their actions. She had excuses for the failings of some teachers and no respect at all for others. "That little English teacher, Ms. Hart, she tries so hard and she's so good, but she just don't know when to clamp down," or, "Now, don't let that gym teacher make you nervous. Her problem is she don't like children no more but she can't afford to retire yet."

Best of all, Pearly was always interested in whatever was on Amanda's mind. Confidences Amanda had only shared with Pink Pig drew thoughtful and often helpful responses from Pearly. "That oral report—what you should do is pick out some kid in the back of the room and tell it to her, like it's between you and her. That way you don't feel like you're talking to so many people, but you don't forget to talk loud. You know what I mean?"

Another thing good about Pearly was that Amanda always knew what she meant. Pearly didn't put fancy covers over what she wanted. "I don't want you visiting my house without your mother and brother knowing, Amanda."

"I always call," Amanda said.

"Strange that your mother don't object to your spending time with me now," Pearly said.

"She has a lot on her mind," Amanda said. She knew she was deceiving both Pearly and her mother, and that

135

it was wrong to enlist Dale to cover for her those times when her call found him at home. She promised herself that soon she would set the matter straight and tell Mother the truth—soon, but not just yet.

One afternoon at the end of October, Amanda carried Flopsy, the fat white rabbit, into Pearly's house and sat stroking the dandelion-fluff fur while Pearly cut a piece of apple pie for her.

"I like apple pie best, especially warm with cinnamon," Pearly said.

"It smells wonderful," Amanda said. It tasted even better. While she ate, Pearly watched her. Pearly's brown eyes had a familiar glow that reminded Amanda of the fond way Pink Pig used to look at her before, when Pink Pig had been able to come alive and wasn't just a glassy figurine squatting stiffly on the miniature shelf. Ever since Amanda had thrown Wizard away, that was all Pink Pig had been. Whatever had happened in the Little World would remain a mystery because without Pink Pig, she had no way of finding out what was going on there. It couldn't be worse without Wizard, she had consoled herself whenever she wondered if she had done the wrong thing by getting rid of him.

"Grandma," Amanda said, and was surprised at the glisten of tears in Pearly's eyes. The "Grandma" had come out by itself. "Grandma," Amanda went on, "did you always work at the school?"

Pearly laughed. "Seems like it, but I was a little girl too once, a very happy little girl. My daddy was a tugboat captain, and I spent a lot of time towing barges up and down the river with him. We lived on the river. I even wound up marrying a river rat. Them wasn't the happiest years. My husband lost his boat and didn't find work that suited him. I had the boy—your daddy—and Tom, my husband, got mean tempered. Wouldn't talk, you know? We moved here because his folks owned this place. It was a little farm then. This kitchen is all that's left of the old place. The rest I built on in bits and starts. Anyway, I went to the school and asked for work and they put me on cleaning. I was glad to have a job there because I could walk home at lunchtime and check on Roland and take care of my in-laws who was ailing. It worked out good."

"Didn't your husband help?"

"Not him. He'd work in the barn—they had a barn out back there with some cows, and we had goats. I liked the goats. You should of seen the old billy goat. That fellow would stand on top of the doghouse and chew off the apples from the lowest branches. Tree's still there, but the apples aren't good for much—wormy. I buy what I need from the farm stand now. Anyways, that old billy goat would follow me around the yard like a dog, and every so often he'd give me a little shove with his head just so I'd remember he was there. He was some character that goat."

"Then what happened to your in-laws?"

"Well, they died, and Tom and me just kept on living here. He was the only son, just like your father. Then one day Tom got struck by lightning. It was in the paper. I still have the article in the photo album. Want to see it?"

Amanda nodded to be polite. Pearly loved any excuse to haul out the photo album, although Amanda had lost interest in the out-of-focus snapshots and yellowed newspaper clippings. "How old was my father when his father got killed?"

Pearly didn't answer immediately. She was busy finding the right page to show Amanda. The newspaper article was faded and hard to read. All it said was that Tom Bickett had been struck by lightning as he was trying to put out a fire that eventually burned down his barn. "How awful," Amanda said.

"Yes," Pearly said. "And your daddy was in high school then, and right after that he joined the army. Well, of course, he was hoping for more opportunity than he'd of had if he'd of stayed around here. Not much chance for a good job without higher education around here, and he wasn't a boy to win any scholarships. Just a good, sweet boy like your brother. Not outstanding in anything."

Amanda was startled to hear her brother referred to as "just a good sweet boy," and she protested, "Dale stands out in sports."

"Well, what I mean is, Dale's part of a team, not the one makes the headlines."

"But Dale *could* win an athletic scholarship, couldn't he?" Amanda asked, thinking of how sure Mother had been until just recently that he would.

"Oh now, I don't know. Maybe he can. I don't know much about it. Does he expect he might?"

"Mother expected him to. Although now she says all he has to do is get in an Ivy League school and she can pay for it. I guess an Ivy League school is the best?" Amanda said, making it a question.

"So I've heard. Well, your mother's smart, and she's

got the ambition. You got to give her credit. Nobody give her any help, and look where she got herself—a nice job in a bank with her own desk and her name on it. I seen it when I went in there once. She looks like something too. I bet you're proud of her."

"Yes," Amanda said. She thought about how her mother looked, and about her craving for beautiful things. Pearly wasn't like that. To be honest, Amanda had to admit that Pearly was homely—clean and neat, but old-fashioned with her barrette of pearls holding the knob of her brown hair in place, with her nose and chin spread too wide in her face. Her belongings were homely too, but she had a sweetness to her. Mother had elegance, and Pearly had sweetness and common sense.

"Then you've been working at the school a long time," Amanda said to encourage more stories.

"I'll say. Been through six principals and all the teachers but Miss Arnold. Miss Arnold been there as long as me, close to thirty-five years. She's going to retire this year, she says."

"And then you'll retire?"

"Oh, not me. They need me in that school. Place would fall apart without me to keep them angels from running wild. Vandalism! You see in the paper all the time how vandalism's a big problem in the school district, but not in my school. Believe you me, I don't let them kids get away with much. They're angels at heart, but if you don't make them behave, they get into mischief. That's how children are.

"Like one year there was a boy, cute little fellow to look at—but he did things like drop frogs in the toilets and tie my mop to the top of the flagpole. Once he spread tar on all the playground equipment. Took me a while to turn *him* around. And do you know, that little fellow still writes me a Christmas card every year? He's grown up now. Lives in L.A. and got a family. Trouble was, his daddy beat him. There's always something when a kid acts up. Never yet found one naturally mean, though we come close."

"Pearly," Amanda said suddenly, "I don't know what I'd do if I didn't have you now that I don't have Pink Pig to talk to anymore."

"You lose that little thing again?"

"No. She's on the shelf. She just doesn't come alive since I got rid of Wizard. I don't know why."

Pearly studied Amanda and said carefully, "You know, that little quartz pig cost a lot more than I thought it should, but I wanted to send you something nice for your birthday, and I didn't have enough for the doll I'd been saving toward, and anyways, I expected your mother probably bought you plenty of dolls. So I figured that maybe a little girl would like a miniature like that . . . I never thought you'd make it real in your head though. I don't know as that's so good, Amanda."

"Pink Pig *is* real," Amanda said. "I didn't make her real."

"Now, is that what you want to believe?" Pearly asked.

"She's my friend," Amanda said stubbornly, "or she was."

"Looks like that chubby little girl you're always with is your friend, and the big one too, the principal's daughter."

Amanda considered. The wall of her belief wavered

140

under Pearly's steady gaze. *Wasn't* Pink Pig real? She had seemed real for so long . . . Amanda fidgeted and stood up. "I ought to be getting home, I guess."

"Sometimes," Pearly said, "people believe things just because they need them so bad. Like I used to believe my son would come home and settle down nearby and I'd have grandchildren come round to hug and make over. Well, my son is gone. Nothing's quite like I believed it would be, but now I'm getting to know you and that means a lot to me. What I'm trying to say, Amanda, is I think you're hanging on to something you don't need anymore."

Amanda kissed the rabbit who was sleeping in her arms. "I'll put Flopsy back in the cage," she said. "Thank you for the delicious apple pie. It's the best I've ever eaten."

"Next time you come, I'll make Dutch apple. Now that's my favorite," Pearly said cheerfully. "And apple cobbler with ice cream. I bet you'd like that."

Pearly wouldn't let her take the late bus. "No sense your riding all 'round town for an hour. I got to pick up some milk at the store anyways. I'll just drop you off home."

The house was so quiet when she walked in that Amanda was sure no one was home. Dale usually had music going if he was there alone, or else there would be sneakers dumped in the living room or schoolbooks discarded on the kitchen table. She went directly to her room and picked up Pink Pig.

"I'm home," Amanda said. "Are you there?" Pink Pig's pinhead eyes looked up at her dotingly. Her snout

141

tilted up and her translucent ears tilted down endearing as ever, but no wriggle of warm flesh showed life in the round pink body, and the corkscrew tail remained a twist of glass. "Come on, Pink Pig," Amanda said. "I believe in you still." The words hung in the air just a shade false. Amanda held Pink Pig to her lips and waited for the cool to turn warm and soften into life while she resisted the doubt that had somehow wormed its way inside her. The quartz warmed against her skin, but nothing else happened.

"Amanda?" The quavering voice was her mother's. "Amanda, where are you?"

"Here," Amanda said. She set Pink Pig down on her dresser and went to her mother's bedroom.

"Come here, my darling," Mother said, and reached out one arm. She was lying on her bed in her stockinged feet wearing the skirt from her gray suit and the high-necked blouse that seemed to be printed with peacock feathers. Her face looked funny. Had Mother been crying?

"What's wrong?" Amanda asked. "Are you sick?" Mother never got sick, never came home from work early, never did anything unpredictable.

"Amanda, oh, Amanda, something terrible has happened."

"What?" Amanda couldn't imagine. "Is Dale all right?"

"Yes. But where is he? He should be home from school by now."

"He probably had something to do," Amanda said.

"But he's supposed to take you with him if he has to go somewhere," Mother said fretfully. "Why—"

"It's okay," Amanda said, impatient with the old deception. "Tell me what happened."

Mother's long thin fingers hid her worried eyes and tear-stained cheeks. "I lost my job," she said in a choked voice. "They fired me."

"Oh," Amanda said. She put her arms tentatively around her mother's shoulders and when Mother clutched at her, Amanda clutched back. "I'm sorry," Amanda said. "I'm very, very sorry for you, but you'll get another job, won't you?"

Mother started crying hard. She pushed Amanda away and buried her face in her pillow. Her shoulders shook with the force of her crying. Amanda was alarmed. "What should I do?" she asked. "Should I call somebody to help you? Do you want me to try to find Dale?"

"No, no. Don't. It's all right. Just—" Mother had raised her head in her effort to reassure Amanda. Now she dropped it and wept again. Amanda stood watching her in helpless horror. "I can't believe it," Mother said. "I felt so certain it would be all right, and I've worked so hard. I deserve some—Oh, Amanda. It's *impossible* that this could be happening to me."

"Libby's father lost his job and he found another," Amanda said, "and I know another girl—"

"Darling, please. I know you mean well, but you don't understand. Just go—See if you can get some dinner together for Dale and send him to me when he gets home, please."

Amanda wished Dale would hurry. He'd know how to comfort Mother. It was frustrating not to know how to help, not to know the right words to say. It must be very

143

hard to get another job if it upset Mother this much to lose hers. Maybe there was only one job like Mother's, the way there was only one principal in the school.

Dale came in limping. "Pulled something in my leg," he said to Amanda. "Wouldn't you know it? The coach said I should—" Mother's voice cut in on him, calling his name.

"Mother's home?" He looked puzzled. "I didn't see her car."

"She got fired," Amanda said. "She's been waiting for you."

His eyes made blue full moons and he rushed off to Mother's bedroom. He closed the door behind him, but a few minutes later Amanda heard him anyway when he began to shout.

". . . could you imagine you could get away with a crazy scheme like that? Are you nuts? You could go to jail."

Amanda put her hands over her ears to shut out the sound of her brother's yelling. The pot of soup began to boil over. When he rushed out of Mother's bedroom, he looked sick.

"Dale," Amanda said. "Please."

"Not now, Mouse, not now. I'll talk to you later." Then he left the house.

She sat down on the couch in the living room and waited. She needed someone to explain things to her, but she didn't know anyone to ask. Her mother's acquaintances were not people Amanda knew. They were just names Mother mentioned, people who worked with her on committees or at the bank. The neighbors weren't friends. The young people in the tiny apartments came and went in less than a year sometimes. On the other side of the street was the house with the old couple who were always traveling and the house where the crazy man lived, and next to that was the social services bureau. Amanda wished she could call Pearly and confide in her.

Pink Pig! Amanda was surprised at herself for not thinking of her friend sooner. She went to her dresser and stroked the smooth round rose quartz back hopefully. "Now. I need you now," Amanda said, and was dismayed when nothing happened.

"Amanda," Mother said from the doorway. She looked very pale and haggard. "Did you hear what Dale and I were talking about?"

"I heard him yelling," Amanda said.

Mother took a deep breath. "Listen," she said. "We're going to move. I told you we needed a new house, remember? Well now, we're going to move to a new town, a big city maybe. You're right. I can get another job. I think I can." She bit her knuckle. "Anyway, we have to get out of here. Tomorrow, instead of going to school, you can help me start packing. We'll pack everything we own, and then we'll call a moving truck and just go. Out West. Somewhere where the sun shines every day. You'll like living out West. You won't have to stay in the house alone when you get home from school anymore. You'll get outdoors and get some sun on your face. Won't that be nice?"

"But I have friends here," Amanda said. "And Pearly—"

"Pearly?" Mother looked confused.

"My grandmother. I don't want to leave her or Libby.

145

And Vera will have to finish the project by herself, and—They won't even know what happened if I go without saying good-bye. Can't we wait a few days, Mother?"

"You can't go to school. It may be in the papers tomorrow."

"What?"

"People will say things to you about your mother. You'll be hurt. I did something, Amanda, something I shouldn't have done. I did it for Dale and for you, because I wanted us to have the good things, the things that matter—Amanda, I *need* you to stay home and help me pack."

She didn't want to pack and she didn't want to leave, but Mother wasn't giving her a choice. Whatever Mother wanted, Amanda had to do. Still she tried. "I don't want to leave," she said again, but Mother turned away as if she hadn't heard.

"Pink Pig," Amanda said softly, but she knew she was alone, all alone, and this time she had no way to avoid the lonelies.

Eleven

"**D**oes Dale happen to be with you? Have you seen
him?" Mother asked as soon as a phone call reached one
of Dale's teammates. The answer always sent her back
to pacing the living room trying to recall yet another
boy's last name. Back and forth, back and forth, in high-
heeled shoes while Amanda watched from the couch.
The only way Amanda could think of helping was to
bring Mother's slippers. "Thank you, darling," Mother
said, but the slippers were useless. No sooner did she
put them on than she sat down at her antique desk and
started pulling out papers and making notes.

It was nearly midnight. Amanda kept expecting
Mother to notice her presence and send her off to bed,
but Mother was unaware of anything except that Dale
wasn't home yet. Tea, Amanda thought. She had just
made a cup when Dale walked in. Quietly Amanda set

the tea on the desk next to Mother's elbow where it cooled unnoticed.

"Dale, where have you *been?*" Mother asked.

"Taking care of some business," Dale said. "Listen, I've thought this thing through. You've got to tell them everything, Mother. You can't hide a penny. You should have accepted as soon as he offered you the deal. They didn't *have* to offer you anything."

"They can't prove I did it. I'm not giving up so easily, Dale. I risked too much and—Amanda!" Mother said. "Why aren't you in bed yet? Look how late it is. You'd better scoot."

"Let her stay," Dale said. "She's going to hear plenty tomorrow in school if it's coming out in the papers."

"She's not going to school. She's going to stay home and help me pack."

"You can't run away from it," Dale said. "They'll come after you. Do you want to spend years in prison?"

"He was bluffing. They're not going to make a scandal out of this. It would be bad publicity for the bank, and he has no proof—except for the one account. If that woman hadn't needed to cash in her investments—Oh, Dale, I was only borrowing it to use now when we need it for your future. It isn't as if I wasn't going to put it all back with interest."

"How and when were you going to manage that?" he asked as if he didn't believe her.

"When they raise my salary to make it commensurate with my title and my responsibilities," she snapped. "Now that's enough. I don't need lectures from you."

"You're crazy if you think they'll just let you walk away and keep any money. Even if they don't go public

148

with it, they'll investigate. They'll find out you've been—"

"Hush," Mother said. Her cheeks were scarlet as she looked at Amanda. "Please, Manda. You want to help me? Please go to bed, darling," she begged.

Amanda took a shower. They were talking in the kitchen when she walked by to get to her alcove. Mother's voice was strained and wobbly. Dale sounded angry. Never had he spoken to Mother in that stern way before. Amanda wondered if it was possible anyone might want to put her mother into jail. People who went to jail were bad, different from anyone she knew. Weren't they? And stealing—could Dale really have meant that Mother stole? It wasn't possible. Amanda sat up gripping her knees and trying to make sense of it all. She was sitting that way when Dale looked into her darkened room.

"Amanda? You awake? Yeah, you are." He came over and sat on the end of the bed without turning on her lamp. "I can't sleep either. Mother went to bed. She's exhausted. I think I talked her into accepting the deal they offered her."

"What deal? She didn't steal anything, did she, Dale?"

"She borrowed money from accounts she manages. She doesn't call it stealing, but the bank will. I don't know, Manda. I thought you were the one in a dream world. It's a shocker to find out Mother's worse. She doesn't understand she could really end up in jail. She won't even believe they'll go public and that it'll get in the paper, but I bet it will. Anyway, she's going to call them first thing in the morning and come clean. She

149

says she can cover what she's spent so far from money she saved up toward my education."

"Then she'll get her job back?"

"No. She's got to go someplace else and start again. Los Angeles maybe. She knows some people out there."

"Do I still have to stay home and help her pack tomorrow?"

"You don't want to go to school, not if anything's in the paper tomorrow."

"Are you going?"

"Yeah. I'm going. I'm going to clean out my locker and say good-bye to a few people . . . I'm not moving to Los Angeles with you, Manda. I'm joining the army."

Amanda caught her breath. "Why?"

"Because that's what's right for me now. I've been tied to Mother's apron strings too long. Besides, if I'd been the hotshot she wanted me to be, she wouldn't have—Anyway, it's time I take charge of my own life. I can make it in the army. I do okay in groups. I bet I'll come out good."

"You're not going to finish high school?"

"Sure I will. I'll take an equivalency exam. Don't you worry about me. I may even be better off this way."

"If you go to the army, you won't live with us anymore." Amanda couldn't bear the thought. "Who will I talk to, Dale?"

He took her hand. "You and Mother—"

"No," Amanda said. "She doesn't think much of me. You're the only one who does—except for Pearly and Libby."

"Listen," he said. "When I'm not around—oh, hey,

Manda, what can I say? I know you get overlooked, but—"

"I don't see why I have to move," Amanda said. "I could live with Pearly and keep going to school."

"You could, but then Mother would be alone."

"*You're* going to be alone."

He thought about it. "Tell you what," he said. "I'll see if I can talk her into letting you go to school tomorrow. You can see how you feel. Who knows? It might even be a good idea for her to go alone at the beginning when she doesn't have a job or a place to live or anything—easier for her to leave you with somebody. Of course, Pearly—Mother's not going to like that much." He patted Amanda's feet. "Go to sleep now," he said, "I'll do what I can for you."

"Dale," Amanda said. "You're my best brother."

"And you're my best sister." He reached over to give her a hug and kissed her. She loved him very much right then.

Mother didn't like it. Mother didn't like it at all, and she was very cross about letting Amanda go to school, even though nothing was in the morning paper about accounts being tampered with at the bank. "I don't see how Pearly got involved in Amanda's life. Didn't I tell you to keep your distance from her, Amanda?"

"I like Pearly," Amanda said. "She's a good person and she loves Dale and me. I didn't want to disobey you, but I didn't know what else to do."

"Dale's gotten close to her too?" Mother asked.

"No, but she kept all his school pictures in an album

and the newspaper clippings about his team winning. You never told me she sent me those birthday presents. I don't see what's wrong with having a grandmother who cares about me."

"As a grandmother, Pearly may be all right, but as a role model, she's a disaster."

"Why?" Amanda asked.

"Her behavior isn't—" Mother caught her breath and touched her fingers to her lips as if she'd thought of something. Amanda wondered if Mother was considering her own recent behavior. "Oh, go to school then," Mother said. "You go, but if anyone says anything to you, ignore them, Amanda. Don't say a word, just hold your head high and ignore them."

"Who's going to know?" Dale asked as he calmly buttered his toast.

"Word gets around fast in a town this small. Someone'll know. Maybe not the children yet, but somebody in the school will have heard. I don't know what ever possessed me to stay here. I should have moved us out of this provincial backwater years ago."

"I'd call the bank president at his home if I were you," Dale said. "Now, before the police start knocking at your door."

Mother stiffened and turned pale. "It's too early," she said. "He'll just be eating breakfast."

"Mother," Dale said softly. "Go make the call. Will you? Please!"

Mother was on the phone when Amanda left to get her bus. She took her regular place toward the middle. Three boys from her class rode the bus, but as usual they ignored Amanda.

In homeroom Libby and Vera were arguing over a book which was overdue at the school library. Libby said she'd lent it to Vera and that Vera had promised to return it on time.

"I did return it. You said I had a week, and I did return it in a week. It's not my fault if you got the date wrong," Vera said.

Libby was angry. "You should pay the fine, Vera," she said. "You get plenty of allowance. All I get's my milk money."

"That's not true. You earn money from your brothers."

"But I spend that on birthday presents for my family."

Amanda waited until Vera walked off in a huff to take the attendance cards to the office. She'd badgered Mr. Whittier into giving her that job. "I never use up my allowance, Libby," Amanda said. "I'll pay the fine for you."

"No," Libby said. "That's not fair. You didn't have anything to do with it. I hate that girl, Amanda. I'm tired of being friends with her."

"We can stop."

"I don't think she'll let go of us until she finds someone else. I wish a new kid would move into our class," Libby said.

"My mother may be moving to Los Angeles," Amanda blurted out.

Libby's mouth fell open. "Oh, no! Manda, you can't do that to me."

"I'm going to ask Pearly if I can live with her," Amanda said. "Don't say anything to anyone, Libby. It's a secret."

Libby looked so miserable that Amanda was sorry she'd warned her. Just then Vera came bustling back into the room. "Amanda," she said. "I heard the secretary in guidance telling about your mother. That's *awful*. You must be so embarrassed."

"Why?" Amanda asked.

"Because your mother robbed the bank."

"Oh, she did not," Libby butted in. "Amanda's mother wouldn't rob a bank. Don't be stupid, Vera."

"She got fired, didn't she?" Vera demanded of Amanda.

"Yes."

"Well, what for?" Vera asked.

"I don't know."

"Yes, you do, but you don't want to talk about it, and I don't blame you. Boy, I'd die if my parents went to jail. I hope your mother doesn't go to jail, Amanda."

"Shut up and leave her alone," Libby said. She looked so fierce Amanda was afraid Libby was going to forget how much bigger Vera was and hit her.

Vera looked hurt. "I'm being sympathetic," she said. "What are you jumping on me for?"

At the end of second period, Amanda got called to the guidance office. She was walking down the hall wondering why, since her appointment with Miss Norris wasn't until the middle of November, when Pearly stopped her. Pearly was wearing her black uniform with the work boots that the kids made fun of. "Amanda, you all right?" Pearly asked.

"I think so," Amanda said.

"I heard about your mother. Can't believe it. I just

can't believe a word of it. Don't let them get to you, honey. You know your mother's innocent."

"No, she's not," Amanda said.

"Terrible the way news gets around," Pearly said. "That guidance office secretary's husband is a manager in the bank and he—" Pearly did a double take. "What did you say?"

"She's going to give the money back though," Amanda said.

"You mean she really took it? Oh, my God!" Pearly slapped her own cheek.

"She's going to move away and get a job someplace else, but I don't want to go," Amanda said.

"You can always come live with me. You know you're welcome," Pearly said, "but I don't expect your mother would let you do that."

"She might," Amanda said.

Pearly smiled at her. "You're something," she said admiringly. "You're really something." She touched Amanda's cheek. "My grandchild," she said proudly. Then she looked both ways to make sure no one was watching and gave Amanda a quick kiss.

Miss Norris scooped Amanda into her office as if she was afraid someone else might grab her first. "Amanda," she said as she dropped into her desk chair and motioned Amanda to sit down too. "I thought you might need to talk to someone this morning. How are you doing?"

"I'm fine," Amanda said.

"You know, I've met your mother? She's a very impressive woman."

"Did I pass the tests?" Amanda asked.

155

"Tests? Oh, I told you not to worry about those, Amanda. I suspect you have a good enough grasp of reality. It's just taking you a little longer to let go of childhood fantasies, that's all. We have an appointment to talk about that, don't we? . . . But I wanted to tell you, you're welcome to share any other problems. You just let my secretary know, and I'll make time for you if I'm in the building. Okay?"

"Okay," Amanda said.

Miss Norris's thin face looked almost pretty when she smiled. "No particular problem you want to talk about this morning?"

"Well," Amanda offered, to oblige her, "my mother wants to move, and I don't want to leave my friends."

"Your miniatures?"

"No, my real friends here in school," Amanda said.

"There you go!" Miss Norris said. "That's a real problem all right. Do you think you'd have trouble making other friends if you moved away?"

"I don't know. But I don't want to leave the ones I have," Amanda said.

"You know what some children who move a lot have told me?" Miss Norris asked brightly. "They say they keep the old friends when they move but add new ones so they end up with more. They say it's fun to come back for visits and have somebody to write letters to. Now that doesn't sound bad, does it?"

"I don't know," Amanda said. "I've never moved before."

"Don't you think it might be an exciting experience?" Miss Norris asked.

Amanda nodded because Miss Norris was trying so

hard to make her feel better. "Anyway, maybe I won't move. Pearly said I can stay with her, and my brother says it might be easier for my mother to move without me."

"Pearly?" Miss Norris looked puzzled.

"Pearly's my grandmother."

"Yes, of course, I'd forgotten," Miss Norris said. "Well, it would be nice to continue seeing you around now that we've gotten to know each other a bit. So I hope you do stay."

By the time Amanda left Miss Norris's office, she felt as if she'd made a new friend without having to move to do it. Miss Norris was nice, and Amanda was glad she thought well of Mother.

She walked back to class wondering if moving could be exciting the way Miss Norris said. Even if it was, Amanda would rather stay. Dale was lucky to be old enough to do what he wanted. She didn't blame him for choosing the army. She just wished she were old enough to make her own choices instead of having to depend on what adults chose for her.

Twelve

Mother had cried, then begged and finally screamed at him, but Dale wouldn't budge. "I know I'm doing the right thing," he said. He sounded so sure and looked so strong that Amanda believed him, but Mother kept trying as they sat over the half-eaten dinner that none of them could finish.

"You're underage," Mother told him. "I can stop you."

"Then I'll just leave home and hole up somewhere until I'm eighteen. That's only a couple more months."

"Why make it hard for yourself?" Mother argued. "Can't you see that if you finish high school first, you'll have a better chance of getting somewhere in the army?"

"I've been struggling to 'get somewhere' all my life, Mother. I'm tired of it," Dale said.

"You mean I've pushed you too hard. Well, if I hadn't

pushed you, you'd be nothing, and you're going to be nothing if you continue to go your own stubborn way."

"Pushing Dad didn't work, why expect it to work on me?" Dale said.

"Dale, you're cruel!" she cried.

"Okay," he said, "but I'll tell you something. I used to feel sorry for Amanda because I got all the attention, but now I think she's been lucky."

"You hate me!" Mother drew back in her chair as if he'd struck her.

He shook his handsome head. "I wish I did, but I love you very much, and that makes it harder for me to break loose. Can't you see that I've got to become my own person?"

Every day Amanda got up in the morning and went to school. She was working alone on the Australia project. Vera had persuaded the teacher to let her join a group of girls who were doing major cities of Australia. Amanda's new subject was kangaroos. She found them interesting and didn't mind working alone. After school she visited Pearly and shared what she'd learned. Pearly marveled with her that the tiny newborn kangaroo could find its own way into its mother's pouch to nurse.

Twice Libby had gone with her to Pearly's house. "I like your grandma a lot," Libby said. She was intrigued with the way the cats and rabbits got along and was delighted when Sonny Boy stepped from the back of the chair onto her shoulder and settled under her ear for a nap. Sonny Boy had been named by Amanda in honor of his deceased mother, Sunny.

159

"Vera wants me to go to the roller skating rink with her Saturday," Libby said one morning, the day before Dale was to leave, "but I told her I wouldn't go unless you were going too. She says she can't be your friend anymore because she's the principal's daughter and your mother is a thief. I told her your mother's not a thief. She just got fired. She didn't have to go to jail or anything. Vera's mean, Amanda. I don't feel sorry for her anymore."

"It doesn't matter what Vera does," Amanda said, "as long as you're my friend." To show how much Libby meant to her, Amanda brought Boy with the Guitar into school and gave him to Libby.

"What's this for?" Libby asked.

"I want you to have him," Amanda said. "He's one of my favorites."

"Thanks," Libby said, and smiled her pleasure.

Vera stuck to the girls with whom she was working on the Australia project. They all liked boys and passed notes back and forth to each other during class about how cute some boy was or who liked whom. The day Amanda gave Boy with the Guitar to Libby, Vera's group had a contest among themselves to see who'd be brave enough to grab a boy and kiss him during lunch. Vera won, but the boy ran to the water fountain and scrubbed his face clean of her kiss. Amanda was embarrassed for her, but Vera didn't act hurt. She laughed and teased the boy by saying if he wasn't nice to her she'd catch him and kiss him again.

"Thank goodness we got rid of her," Libby said.

Amanda worried about how Libby would manage

160

without her in school if Mother wouldn't leave her with Pearly.

That night, Amanda and Mother took Dale to the bus. Mother had finally signed the permission form for Dale to join the army and he was leaving for boot camp. Amanda expected Mother to be awash in tears, but Mother surprised her. She wore the blue wool dress that Dale said matched her eyes, and her soft cashmere coat. Dale drove the old car. When he walked around to the passenger side to let Mother out, she gave him a big smile and a kiss and said, "Best of luck, my darling."

"Aren't you going to wait with me until my bus leaves?" Dale asked.

"You know I'm not good at good-byes."

He looked disappointed, but he said, "All right then. Take care of yourself. And be sure to send me your new address as soon as you get one." He kissed her again. Then while she slid over to the driver's side, he helped Amanda transfer from the back to the front seat. But before she got in, he picked her up and hugged her hard.

"You going to write me?" he asked huskily.

She nodded, too choked to talk.

"You know, I'm going to miss you a lot, Manda," he said.

"Me too," she squeaked. "I'm going to miss you, Dale."

She clung to him until Mother said sharply, "Amanda, get into the car now."

"Bye, sweetheart. Good luck," Dale said.

Amanda sat down beside Mother who put her smile back on and waved at Dale. Then she drove away. It

161

wasn't until she stopped at the next traffic light that the tears began to roll down her cheeks in a sad silent stream which hurt Amanda to watch.

"Let's go to the mall," Mother said. "I don't feel like going back to the house yet."

Amanda didn't say anything. She felt strange being alone with Mother, just the two of them without Dale to wait for or feed or buy something for. What would happen to them all? If Pink Pig were alive—but Pink Pig had been nothing but a small rose quartz figure on her miniature shelf for weeks now. Amanda shivered. Pearly could comfort her, but Mother would never approve of that. Nor was she likely to leave her daughter behind with a person she despised. She would move Amanda along with the furniture to California. No doubt she would. And running away wouldn't work, because where could Amanda run to? She couldn't manage on her own yet like Dale. She was just too young.

They walked in the mall. Mother stopped in front of the shoe store window. "You could use dressy shoes," she said. "I wish I could buy you those pumps with the bow. What do you think, Amanda?"

"Nice," Amanda said, "but I don't need them." She didn't want new shoes.

"Dale always hated shopping," Mother said. "Do you like to shop, Amanda?"

"Sometimes," she said, wary of displeasing Mother.

"Are you just saying that or do you mean it? Or don't you *know* what you like?" Mother asked irritably.

"I know what I like," Amanda said.

"Then why don't you ever tell me? How do you expect me to understand you if you won't tell me how you feel?"

"I'm sorry," Amanda said.

"Do you talk to Pearly?"

"Yes."

"And I suppose she understands you."

Amanda tried to make it all right. Cautiously, so as not to hurt Mother more than she was already hurting from Dale's departure, Amanda said, "It's okay if you like Dale better than me. I love him a lot too."

"Do you love *me* at all?" Mother asked childishly.

"Well," Amanda said. "You're my mother." Mother waited for Amanda to say more, but she couldn't think what to add.

"And Pearly?" Mother asked. "Do you love her too?"

"Yes," Amanda said.

"Why?"

"Because—" Amanda searched through all the reasons she loved Pearly for one that was neutral. Because Pearly loved her as she was, because Pearly was kind and cheerful, because Pearly didn't want to change everything. It was better not to finish the "because," Amanda decided.

"Amanda," Mother said, sitting down on a bench between a lily-shaped wastebasket and a potted tree that reached up for the skylight in the ceiling of the mall. "Dale thinks the best I can do for you is to leave you here with your grandmother when I go to Los Angeles. I can't agree with him. I've made a mistake, but that doesn't make me an unfit mother." Her back was straight but her voice was thin as she continued. "I think I can provide a better background for you than a person like Pearly who has no appreciation for the finer things of life. She's no role model for you. She's—Say

163

something, Amanda. If you'd talk to me, we might begin communicating. It drives me up a wall to have to guess at what you're thinking."

"Pearly spends time with me," Amanda explained cautiously. "She likes to talk with me, and I like to be with her. She has kittens and rabbits, and she makes kids behave themselves, but she loves them, and some of them like her and come back to the school to visit her. She works hard, like you do, but she just tries to do a good job. She doesn't expect to get promoted or be better than anybody. She's a good person."

"And I'm not?"

"You're a good person too, but you try too hard," Amanda said. She would have added, "and you don't hear what I tell you," but it seemed that Mother was trying to listen now.

Mother was silent for a long time. Then she said, "I'll call Pearly and see if I can visit her."

"She doesn't have a phone," Amanda said. "But she's always home except to go to the store. We could drive over and see if she's there."

Amanda couldn't believe it when Mother agreed. They stopped at the florist's booth. "I'll bring her a peace offering," Mother said. "What do you think she would like?"

Amanda chose a nosegay of straw flowers. It wasn't expensive, and she could see Mother didn't think much of it. "These will keep," Amanda said. "Pearly's practical, and she'd like something that would last."

Mother sighed and bought a fancier arrangement of straw flowers in a basket. "We'll go tomorrow," Mother said. "I'm too exhausted now."

At home Mother walked through the living room, which looked bare with everything but the big furniture and one lamp packed away for the move to Los Angeles. She went to her own room and closed the door. Amanda heated chicken gumbo soup and left a bowl out and half the soup in the pot for Mother. Pearly would probably like the straw flowers, which were the gold and wine and cream colors of Indian corn. It would be so much better to stay with Pearly than to go to Los Angeles, but Amanda tried not to build her hopes too high.

Mother looked at Pearly's house with distaste. Smoke was coming out the chimney. Amanda sniffed the sweet burning cherry wood and was glad to see Pearly's rusty blue car parked by the woodshed. The plaster ducks looked cold on the browned-over lawn. Even though the sky was blue, the air had a November bite. Mother had a smile ready when Pearly opened the door.

"Surprise!" Mother said as coolly as if they often came for a visit.

"Well, look who's here," Pearly said. "Come on in. I was just doing some ironing in the kitchen. Wait a second and let me clear these uniforms off the chairs."

"Don't fuss for us," Mother said. "We just came to say hello." She held out the white box. "This is for your kindness to Amanda."

"What kindness?" Pearly looked flustered. She took the ribbon-tied box and set it on the table as if she didn't know what to do with it. "It's been some treat, let me tell you, to get to know my granddaughter. You raised a wonderful little girl here. You can be real proud of her."

"Thank you," Mother said. She sat down on the chair

165

at the kitchen table from which Pearly had whisked two black ironed uniforms.

"Let me get you something to drink . . . coffee?" Pearly asked hopefully.

"Oh, yes, thank you," Mother answered, and crossed her legs. Her eyes made a survey of the cluttered kitchen. To Amanda, Mother looked as out of place there as a cockatoo in a henhouse, even though she wore a plain skirt and sweater with her usual high heels. Amanda only hoped Mother saw how clean the kitchen was.

"Amanda, you want to set out the cups, lamb?" Pearly asked. Amanda got to work, glad of something to do. She found paper napkins and folded one for each place at the table. Pearly usually didn't bother with napkins, but Mother would expect them.

Pearly made hot chocolate from an instant mix for Amanda and chatted with Mother about the rabbits, one of which was hunkered down between two sleeping cats in a box near the stove. ". . . Mostly keep them out in the winter, but the cats got so used to them. I'm thinking maybe it won't harm nothing to bring them in, at least, when it's down below freezing. They're good company, the rabbits. Aren't they, Amanda?"

Amanda picked up Mopsy, who settled like a cushion on her lap. Sonny Boy leaped onto her lap too and treaded against her thigh, pressing down one paw and then the other as he searched for the ideal resting place.

"Animals make such a mess in the house," Mother said. "You must be cleaning up after them all the time."

"Oh, I don't mind cleaning," Pearly said. "Consider-

166

ing how long I've been at it, be too bad if I did." She laughed.

"Good coffee," Mother said.

"Guess I'll open my present," Pearly said when nobody added anything to the conversation. "I don't get presents as a rule. Makes me feel like a kid opening this one. When I was little, I had to open my birthday presents in front of everybody like this. Always embarrassed me." She had taken the ribbon off and now she lifted the basket of dried flowers out. "Now, what a pretty thing! Won't this make my table look elegant." She placed it right in the center, pushing aside a sugar bowl and salt and pepper shakers. "Thank you," she said. "That's really nice."

"Amanda picked it," Mother said. "She said you'd like something that would last. She seems to know a lot about you."

"Yes, well, her and me have been getting along good," Pearly said. She hesitated. "You know," she said. "I've been thinking how things are. If you'd be willing to leave her with me until you get settled where you're going—well, it'd be a treat for me to have her for a while."

"You're very kind," Mother said. She looked around uneasily.

"This house is small, but Amanda could have her own room," Pearly said eagerly. "See, I made Roland's room into a storeroom, but I could move my sewing machine and the spring bulbs out and heat it easy enough. Want me to show you?"

Mother gave an edgy little smile and said, "Amanda

says you have a photograph album with Dale's school pictures in it."

"I sure do. Come in the next room, why don't you, and we'll sit on the sofa and go through it." Pearly acted as if she were making progress. Amanda wasn't so sure.

They moved into the living room and again Mother's eyes traveled carefully over the clutter. Amanda saw a spiderweb in the corner of the window. She hoped Mother didn't notice it.

"Amanda told me you wouldn't mind taking care of her temporarily," Mother observed as she flipped through the pages of the photograph album.

"Amanda's my grandchild. She's always welcome here."

"You know I'm relocating. I'm moving to Los Angeles in a few days," Mother said, pushing every word out with difficulty. "It's a move that hasn't been—well, I don't even have an apartment out there yet. It's true that while I'm getting settled, it might be easier for Amanda to stay here with you and continue attending the school she's accustomed to. Then I can send for her as soon as I have things arranged."

"She's welcome as long as you'll let her stay. It'll be a treat to me to have her, believe you me, and I'll take good care of her and do the very best I can for her." Pearly seemed breathless with excitement.

"I don't know how long. It might take me a while. That is, jobs being something one can't predict—" Mother bit her lips and looked upset.

"She could write you every day," Pearly said. "She'd let you know just how she's doing. And it'll be a lot easier for you to get set up without a little girl to worry about out there."

"Yes," Mother said, in control of herself again. She looked at Amanda. "Unless you'd rather come with me?"

"I'll write you," Amanda said and kissed Mother's cheek. "Thank you so much." That was when Mother abruptly burst into tears.

A few days later, Amanda was unpacking her belongings in the room that used to be her father's. Pearly had cleared it of everything except a bed and dresser. Before she went to bed, Amanda hung her miniature shelf on a nail on the wall. She unwrapped all the figures, including Wizard's coach, and set them in their stations. Pink Pig was last. Amanda was holding her, yearning for Pink Pig to come to life again, when Pearly came into the room.

"You warm enough, honey?"

"Yes, fine, Grandma."

"Well, hop in bed and I'll give you a kiss good night," Pearly said.

Amanda did as she was told. Being tucked in made her feel babyish, but nice this first night away from home. "Want the light on?" Pearly asked.

"No, thank you. I like the dark," Amanda said. Pearly blew her another kiss and turned off the light. Amanda put Pink Pig under her pillow and closed her eyes. "Pink Pig," she whispered. "Please, I need you."

"There you are," Pink Pig said. "You're just in time for the circus."

"What circus?" Amanda asked.

"They've all come out of hiding," Pink Pig said. "Come on. Everyone's going, everyone but Boy with the Guitar."

"I gave him to my friend Libby," Amanda said. "He'll be happy with her."

"As long as he has his music, Boy with the Guitar's happy," Pink Pig agreed. "Come on. Everyone will be glad to see you. We never had a chance to thank you for saving our world."

"Did I save it, Pink Pig?"

"Come see for yourself," Pink Pig said.

They were standing together on the endless road which disappeared into the distance. On either side of them were green fields glowing with sunshine. Amanda could hardly believe it. "It's all changed back again," she said.

"Yes," Pink Pig said. "Since you got rid of Wizard, everything's begun to grow and bloom again. The birds and deer are feeding in the woods, and Frog can fill up on flies without leaving his lily pad. Peasant Man and Peasant Woman are busy packing the harvest into the barn, but today they're all in town to see the circus. Look." Pink Pig pointed up toward the hill where Wizard had once lived. The veils of mist were still gone and Amanda saw ruined castle walls already half covered with vines.

"I'm so glad," Amanda said with relief.

The first creature Amanda saw as they approached the town square was Spangled Giraffe, whose head reached the peak of the skinny one-story houses. Everyone was watching Ballerina twirling in the center on a wooden stage while Clown made music on a xylophone for her.

As soon as Ballerina had finished, Pink Pig called, "Here she is, the one who saved us." Everyone turned toward Amanda. Peasant Man bowed and Peasant Woman curtsied, and each took one of Amanda's hands and led her onto the stage where she stood shyly while Ballerina and Clown and every creature with hands clapped for her.

"She threw the Wizard out. Let us all give a shout. Oh, hip, hip, yay hooray. For us she saved the day," Frog croaked. While Clown did back flips all around the edges of the stage, Peasant Girl tossed out flowers from her baskets, and Wild Horse reared onto his hind legs neighing. Then the knight with the Viking horns on his helmet opened the door of the gold and red coach and the knight in armor bowed ceremoniously to Amanda and led her to it. She sat on the velvet cushions while they drove her around the square in a triumphant procession.

First came the coach, followed by Wild Horse, and next came Brass Elephant and Spangled Giraffe. Pink Pig acted as ringmaster for the birds, who performed a curious dance in the air above the stage, while the sun shone on a world as busily alive as it had been before Wizard changed it to suit himself.

When the celebration was over and everyone had gone, Amanda was left alone with Pink Pig. "I'm glad the Little World is well again, and especially glad to find you again, Pink Pig," Amanda said.

Pink Pig fixed her inky eyes fondly on Amanda and said, "Yes, it was good to say good-bye."

171

"Good-bye?"

"You know that you don't need me anymore," Pink Pig said wistfully.

"But I'm not sure," Amanda protested.

"You're sure," Pink Pig said. "You don't need magic now. You're brave and you can help yourself."

"Yes, I know, but—"

"But?"

"But suppose I need a friend?" Amanda asked.

"You have plenty of human friends now," Pink Pig said.

It was true, Amanda thought. With Pearly and Libby and Mother and Dale and Miss Norris and the kittens and rabbits to spend time on, her life was very full. "But—" Amanda said.

"Buts will make it harder, you know," Pink Pig said. "Why don't you just say good-bye."

Amanda opened her mouth, but she was too choked to speak.

"Good-bye my dear dear friend, good-bye," Pink Pig said. Slowly her stubby snout and her translucent ears and even her plump body and corkscrew tail hardened into glassy quartz until the only life remaining in her was the love in her pinpoint eyes.

"Amanda," Pearly called. "Come taste my pancakes. Your father used to say I made the best buttermilk pancakes in town. And I got real maple syrup for you."

Amanda sat up in bed. It was morning and she was still holding Pink Pig in her hand. A fat sunbeam made a dusty radiance from her window to the foot of her bed.

172

Amanda got up, put on her slippers and robe and set Pink Pig back on the miniature shelf. Last night it seemed Pink Pig had come alive again in a most spectacular dream in which Amanda had been applauded by all the miniatures on the shelf. This time she knew she'd been dreaming, and yet, it did seem that something had happened because she felt different, sure of herself and confident about the future.

"I'm coming, Grandma," Amanda said, and went off to eat her pancakes. She would have mentioned her dream to Pearly, but she didn't have time with so much to do before setting off to school There were the breakfast dishes to clean and the cats to let out, and the rabbits needed drops put in their eyes because they had eye infections.

That evening Amanda was cutting a skirt from a pattern she had picked for herself. Pearly was teaching her how to sew.

"Did you write to your mother and brother yet?" Pearly asked.

"I wrote to Dale in school because I finished my math early. I'll write to Mother tomorrow."

"Might be a good idea if you kept writing her every day, Amanda. She'll be lonely out there all by herself."

"She's staying with her friend."

"Her friend's not her family."

"Dale's the one she wants to hear from," Amanda said.

"I bet your letters make her happy too."

"All right," Amanda said. "I'll write her before I go to bed. I'll tell her about learning to sew. She'll be surprised."

"And the party you're going to Saturday with Libby. Don't forget that," Pearly said.

Amanda got in bed with the box of stationery Pearly had bought her. Writing to Mother was much easier than talking to her had ever been.

"Soon it may snow," she wrote. "Snowflakes are pretty. I hate being cold, but I like going inside and getting warm, and I love fires in the stove and the smell of cooking. I'm hoping that you find a job soon and that you don't get lonely. It will be so nice when you and Dale and I can see each other again, but meantime I'm having a good time here and hope you are really okay too. . . ."

Sonny Boy jumped up on Amanda's bed and curled against her legs. As Amanda sat propped on her pillow writing page after page of all her thoughts and feelings, Sonny Boy purred.

Christmas was coming closer. Amanda had a role in her class's play for the Christmas assembly. She was one of the children who put food on the tree for the forest animals. Pearly was going to the play, but Mother and Dale couldn't. Mother had hoped to come back East for Christmas, but she didn't have the money because she hadn't found a job yet. She sounded worried in her letters, and Amanda tried to cheer her up in hers. Just recently she'd written to Mother: "You'll find a job very soon. I know you will because you're smart and you work hard and you're beautiful."

And Mother wrote back: "I think you like me better at a distance, Manda. You never gave me compliments

174

before. Believe me, I cherish them and will save your letter to reread whenever I feel blue."

Dale wrote that army life was easy and kind of fun in a way. "I'm good at most of the stuff they make us do, which feels great for a change. Guess what Mother wrote me about you? She said she's getting to know you better from your letters than she ever did when we lived together. She seems to be having a rough time getting a job, and I hope you really are as happy with Pearly as you sound, because it looks as if you'll be there a lot longer than Mother thought. She misses you, Amanda. Maybe it's good for us all to be separated for now, but I'm looking forward to my first leave when I'll try hard to visit you. Thought that might be Christmas, but it doesn't look like it. You'll be all grown up and beautiful by the time I see you next. Can't wait."

One night Pearly watched Amanda staring out into the snowflake-streaked darkness while she stroked the gray cat asleep in her lap. "You feeling sad, honey?" Pearly asked.

"I'm fine," Amanda said although she *was* feeling down.

"We'll have a nice Christmas together," Pearly said. "It'll be something for me to have family here. Been a long time since I ate Christmas dinner with family."

Amanda smiled at that, but she said, "Mother will be alone this Christmas."

"Poor lady," Pearly said. "She's having a rough time of it, isn't she?"

"I hope she gets the cookies I sent her, and the pine cones we made. Do you think she'll like them?" Amanda asked uncertainly. They were sprayed with gold and stuck with silver stars. Mother might think they were tacky.

"She'll like that they come from you," Pearly said.

That night when Pearly came into Amanda's room to kiss her good night, Amanda was lying awake in the moonlight. "Want me to pull down the shade, angel?"

"No, I like the moonlight," Amanda said.

"You still feeling bad about your mother?"

"I was thinking," Amanda said, "about sending her Pink Pig for Christmas."

"Well now, that might be just the thing to cheer her up," Pearly said. "But won't you feel bad giving that miniature away? I thought it was your favorite."

"It is," Amanda said. "That's why I want to send it." Tomorrow, she decided, she would pack Pink Pig well and mail her off to Mother. Even if Pink Pig didn't come alive for Mother, the gift might please her, and bring her some magic, or at least enough love to ward off the lonelies.